Sports Illustrated KIDS
GRAPHIC NOVELS

STONE ARCH BOOKS
a capstone imprint

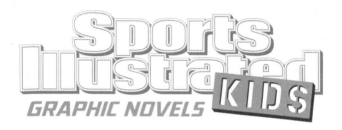

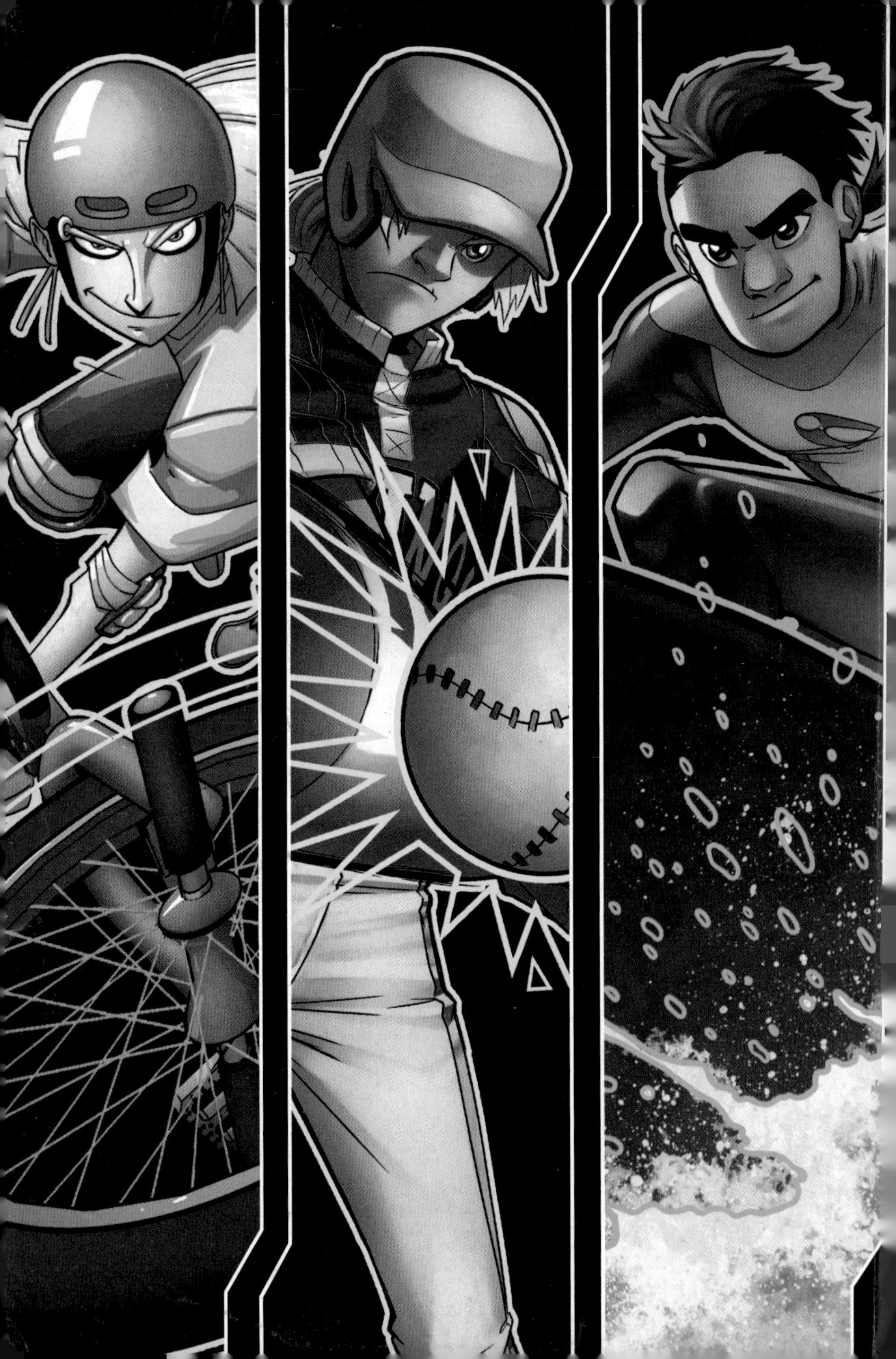

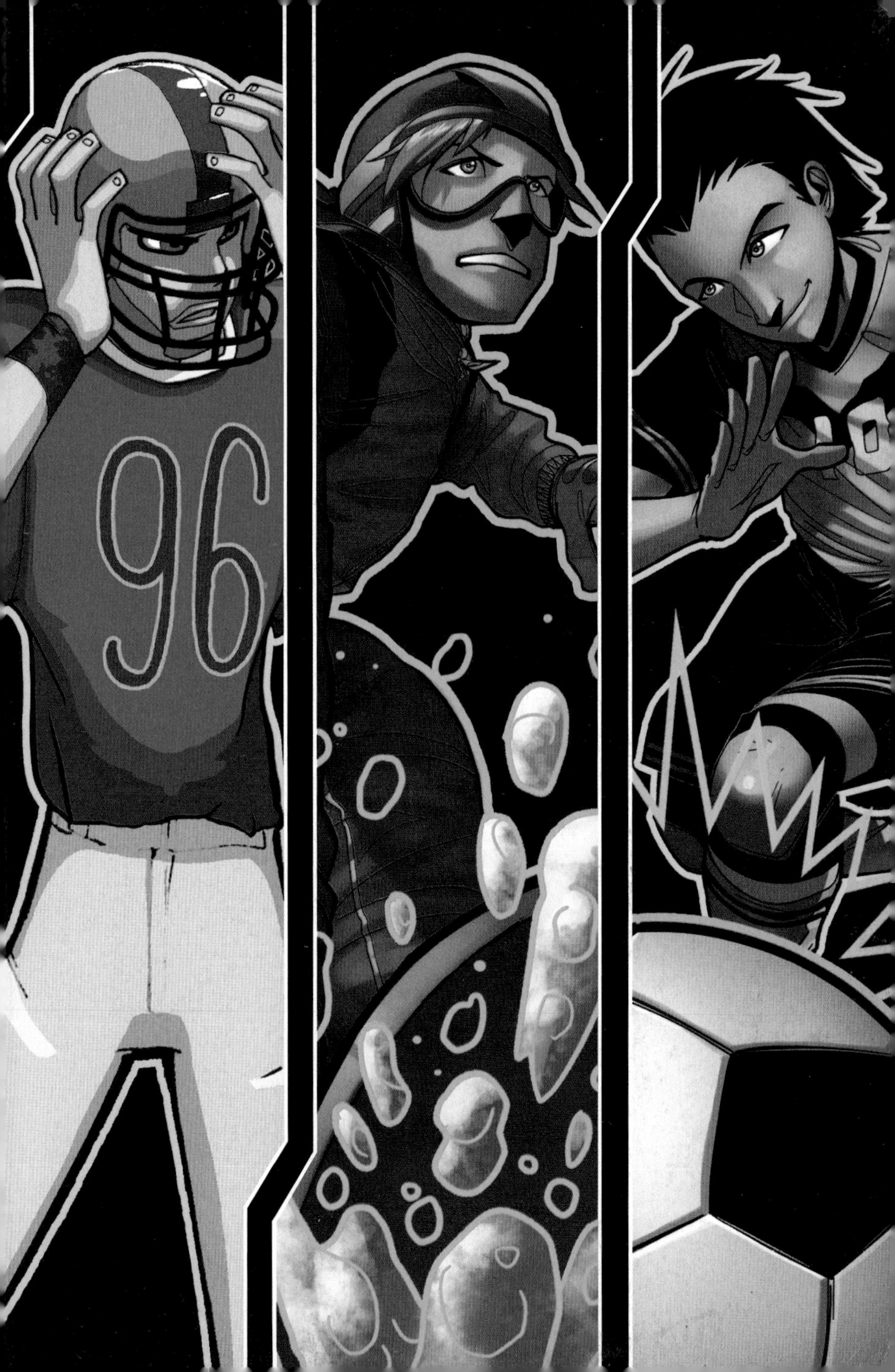

UP NEXT ›››

Sports Illustrated KIDS

:02 SPORTS ZONE SPECIAL REPORT

:04 FEATURE PRESENTATION:

SNOWBOARD STANDOFF

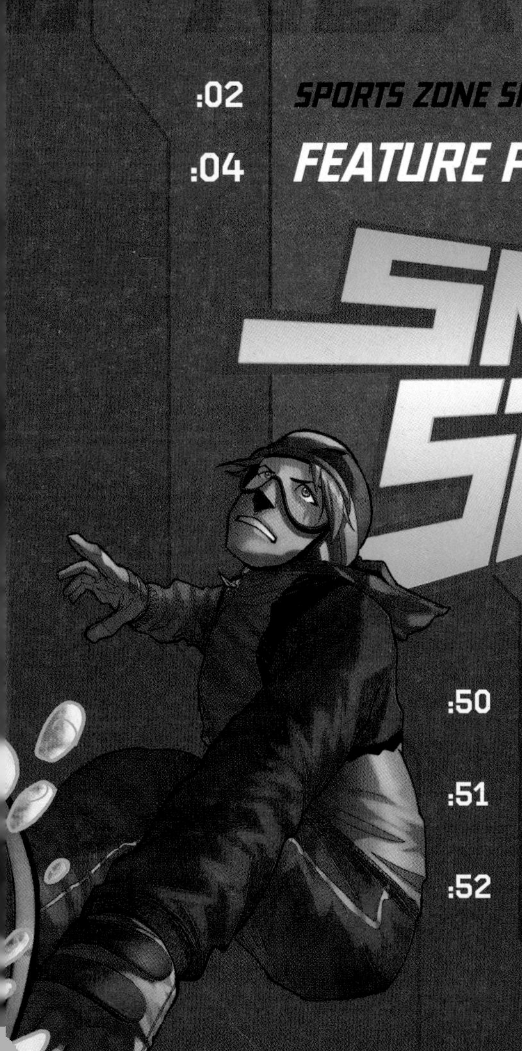

FOLLOWED BY:

:50 SPORTS ZONE POSTGAME RECAP

:51 SPORTS ZONE POSTGAME EXTRA

:52 SI KIDS INFO CENTER

TEAM ROGUE READY AND RARING TO GO AS TEAM ALHPA ARR SIK TICKER

SPORTS ZONE
SPECIAL REPORT

SNO SNOWBOARDING
PNT PAINTBALL
SKT SKATEBOARDING
BMX BMX FREESTYLE
SRF SURFING

THREE TOP TEAMS MEET IN FREESTYLE TOURNAMENT

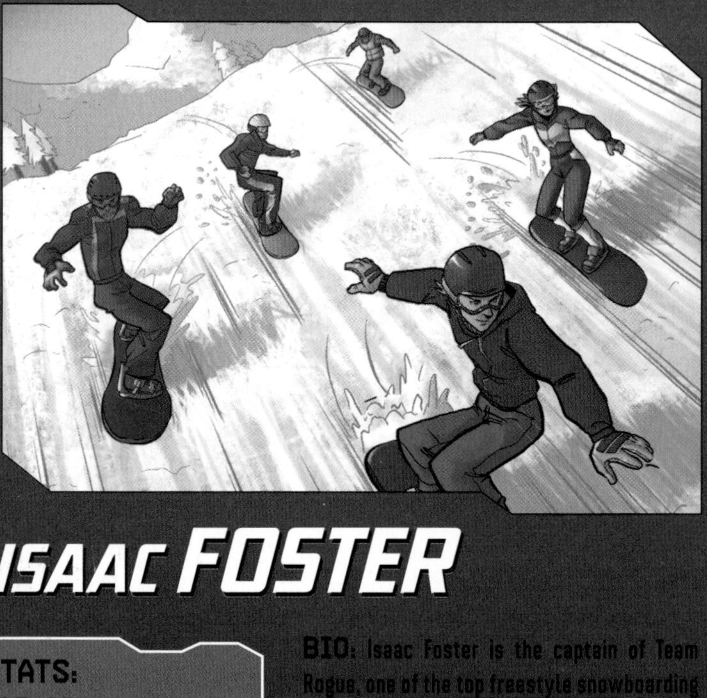

ISAAC FOSTER

STATS:
AGE: 14
SQUAD: TEAM ROGUE

BIO: Isaac Foster is the captain of Team Rogue, one of the top freestyle snowboarding teams in the entire country. Isaac believes there is a "best" way to snowboard, and he expects his teammates to achieve a perfect understanding of the basics of the sport. If he wants to beat Teams Alpha and Blitz, his entire squad will have to be at the top of their game.

Sports Illustrated KIDS

UP NEXT: SNOWBOARD STANDOFF

BLZ vs BKS 3-1
TGR vs RDR 33-32
EAG vs BAN 14-7
SPA vs WLD 4-3
BAN vs RDR 21-15
RZR vs LIG 4-1
BLZ vs BKS

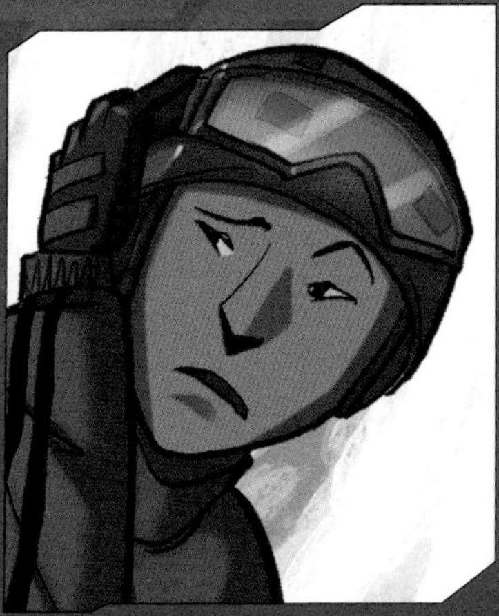

KAI PALAKIKO

AGE: 14 | SQUAD: TEAM ROGUE

BIO: Kai is a former surfer from Hawaii who loves the water and waves there. Unfortunately, Kai and his family recently moved. Now, with no waves in sight, Kai hopes to take on the snow and slopes to test his athletic abilities.

BRYAN FOSTER

AGE: 14 | SQUAD: TEAM ALPHA

BIO: Bryan thinks he's the best snowboarder around — and he might be right — but he doesn't care about anyone but himself.

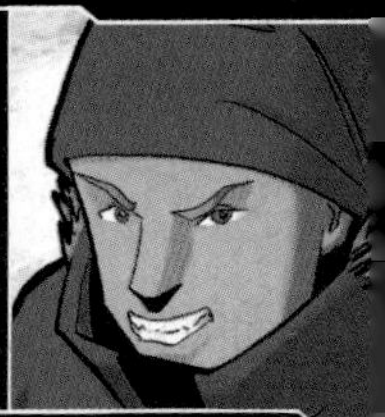

MONA DARE

AGE: 14 | SQUAD: TEAM ROGUE

BIO: Mona is a talented shredder — and as sarcastic as they come. She has a smart remark ready for any given situation.

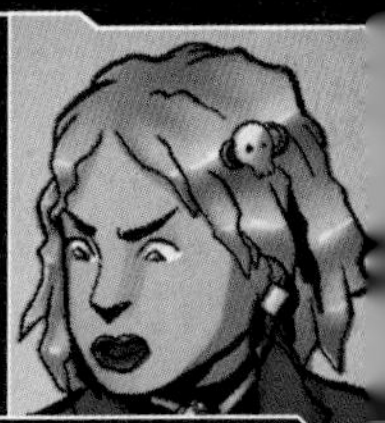

TEAM ALPHA

BIO: Team Alpha, led by Bryan Foster, has some of the best boarders around. They win most tournaments they enter, and they aren't afraid to brag.

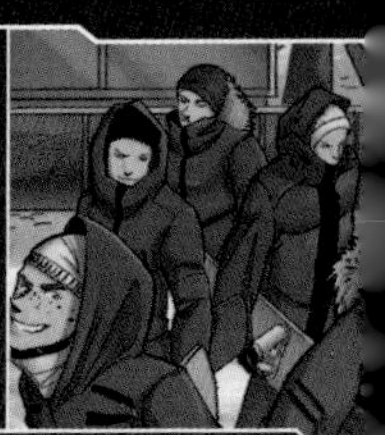

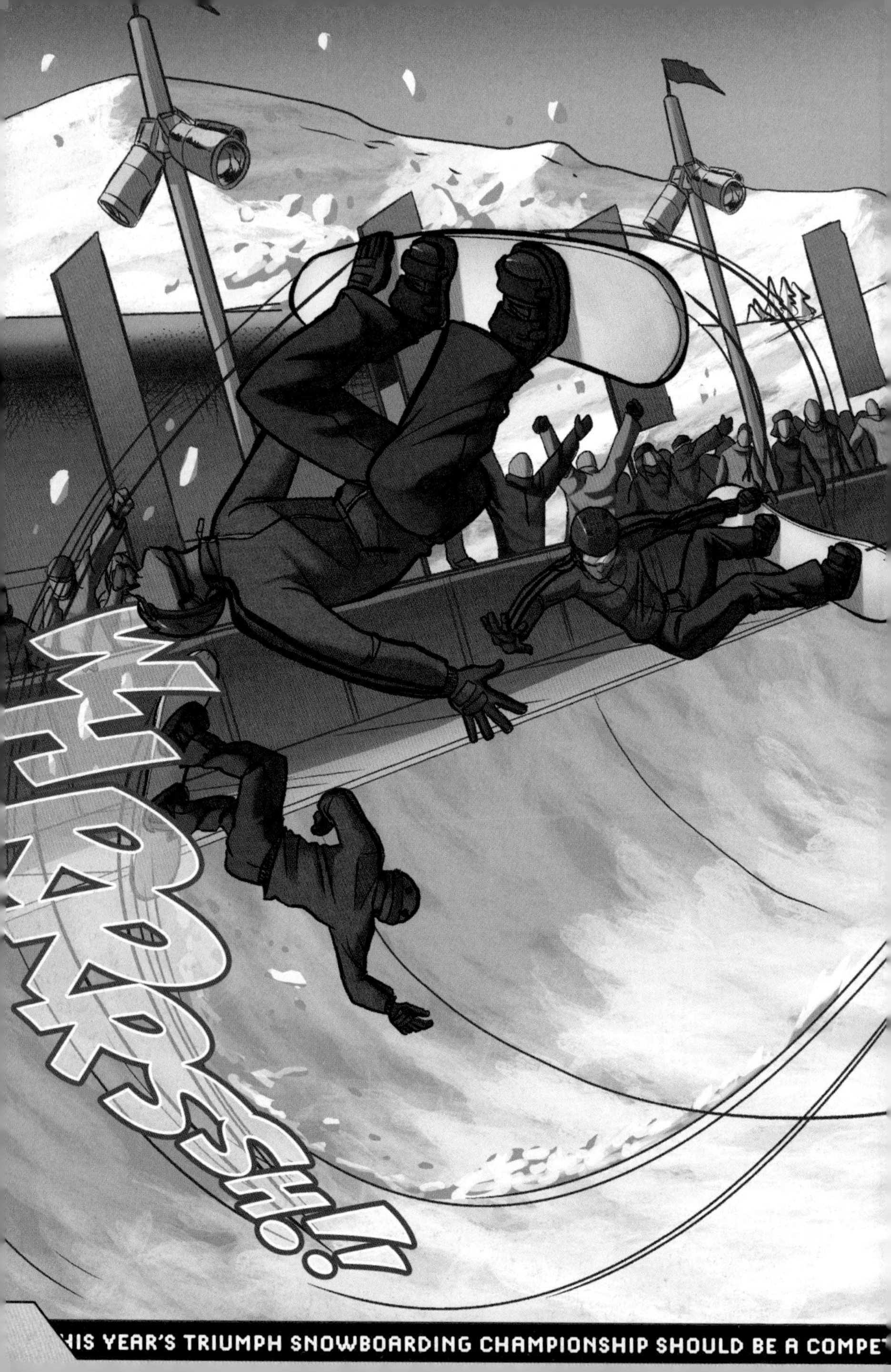
WHRRRSSH!!
HIS YEAR'S TRIUMPH SNOWBOARDING CHAMPIONSHIP SHOULD BE A COMPE

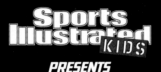

Sports Illustrated KIDS

PRESENTS

SNOWBOARD STANDOFF

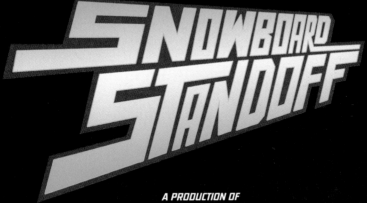

A PRODUCTION OF

STONE ARCH BOOKS
a capstone imprint

written by Scott Ciencin
penciled by Fabian Cobos
inked by Sergio Martinez
colored by Fernando Cano

designed and directed by Bob Lentz
edited by Sean Tulien
creative direction by Heather Kindseth
editorial management by Donald Lemke
editorial direction by Michael Dahl

Sports Illustrated KIDS *Snowboard Standoff* is published by Stone Arch Books,
1710 Roe Crest Drive, North Mankato, Minnesota 56003.
www.capstonepub.com

Summary: Kai Palakiko is an open-minded former surfer who believes adaptability is key to snowboarding success. But on Isaac's team, you either fall in line, or you fall by the wayside.

Cataloging-in-Publication Data is available at the Library of Congress website.

ISBN: 978-1-4342-2242-8 (library binding)
ISBN: 978-1-4342-3403-2 (paperback)

Printed in the United States of America in Stevens Point, Wisconsin.
052012 006764R

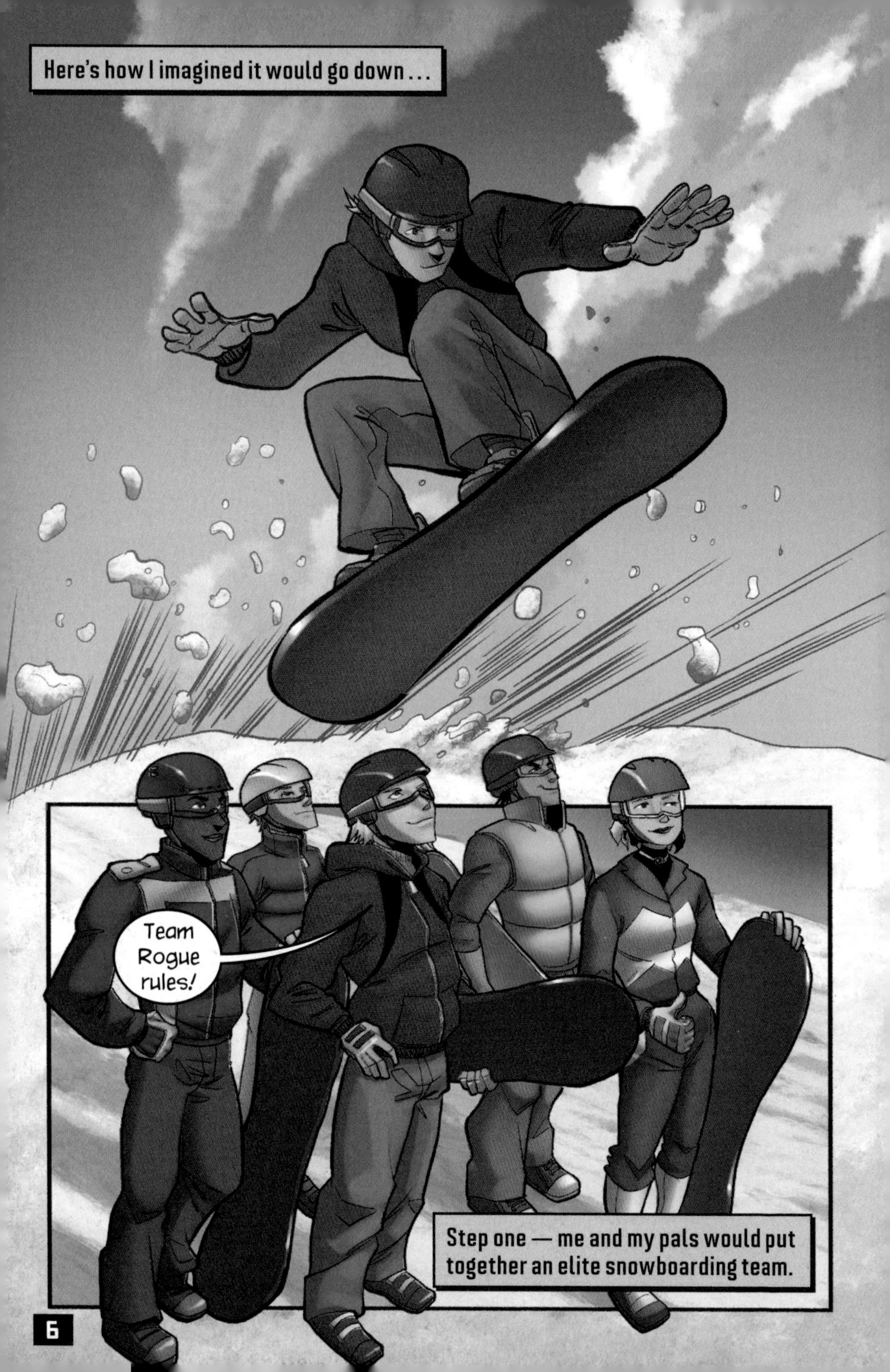

Here's how I imagined it would go down . . .
Team Rogue rules!
Step one — me and my pals would put together an elite snowboarding team.

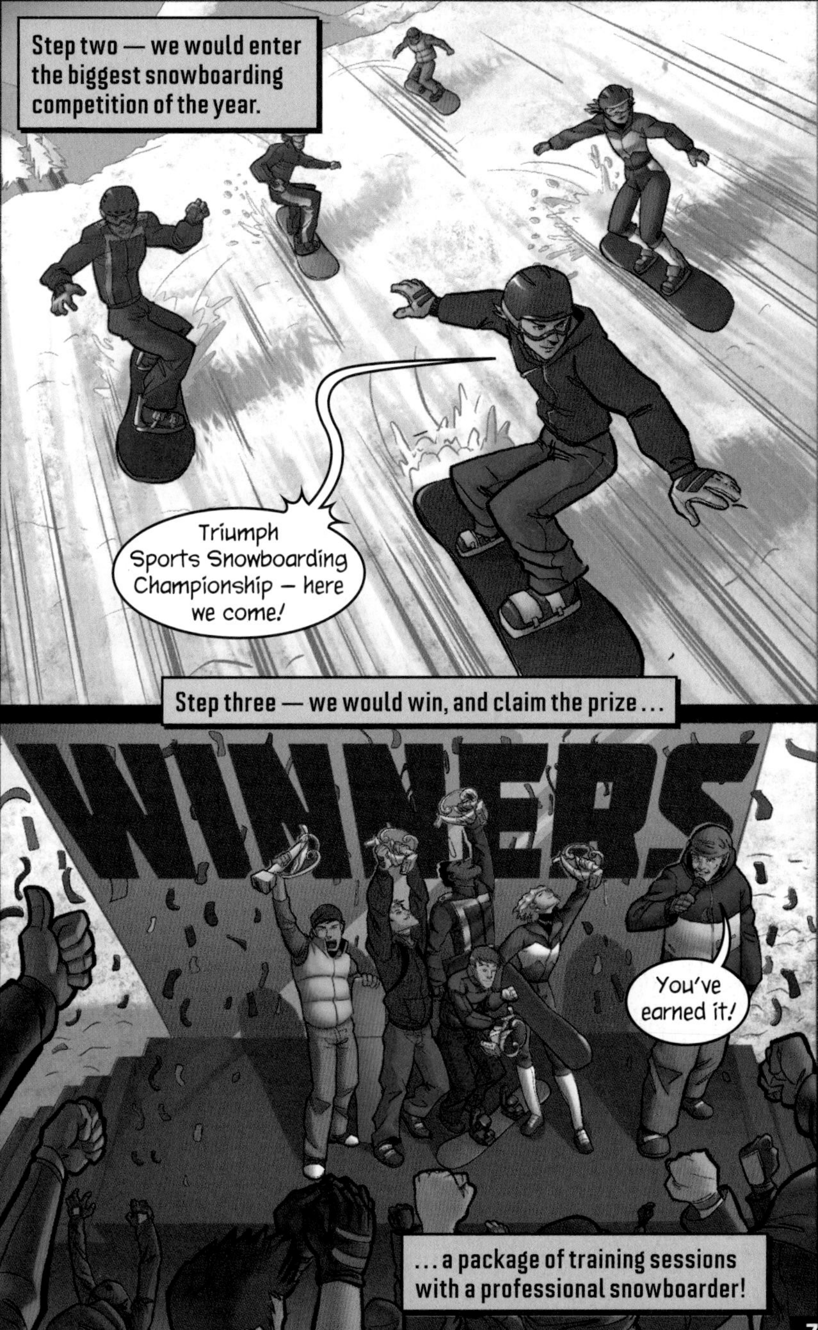
Step two — we would enter the biggest snowboarding competition of the year.
Triumph Sports Snowboarding Championship — here we come!
Step three — we would win, and claim the prize . . .
WINNERS
You've earned it!
. . . a package of training sessions with a professional snowboarder!

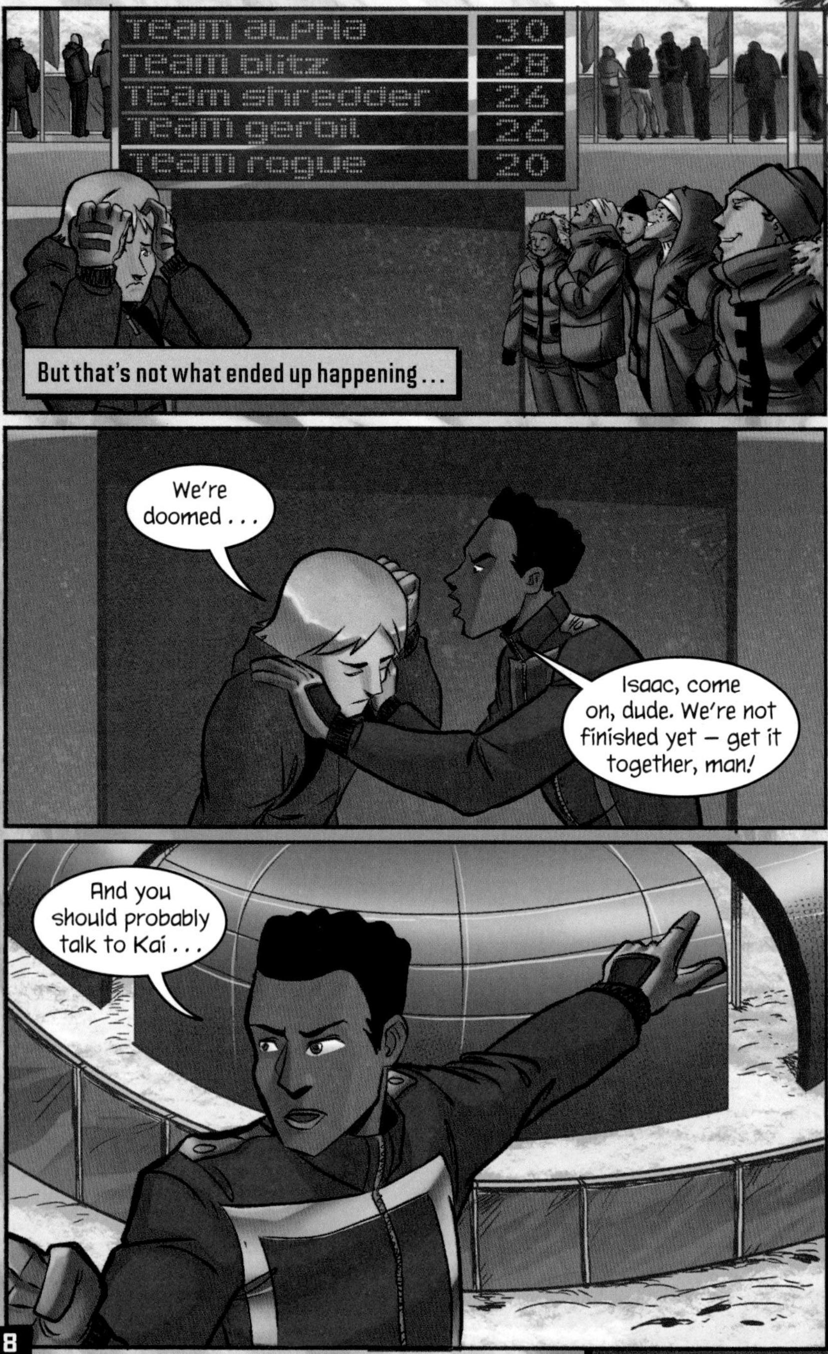
TEAM ALPHA 30
TEAM BLITZ 28
TEAM SHREDDER 26
TEAM GERBIL 26
TEAM ROGUE 20
But that's not what ended up happening . . .
We're doomed . . .
Isaac, come on, dude. We're not finished yet — get it together, man!
And you should probably talk to Kai . . .

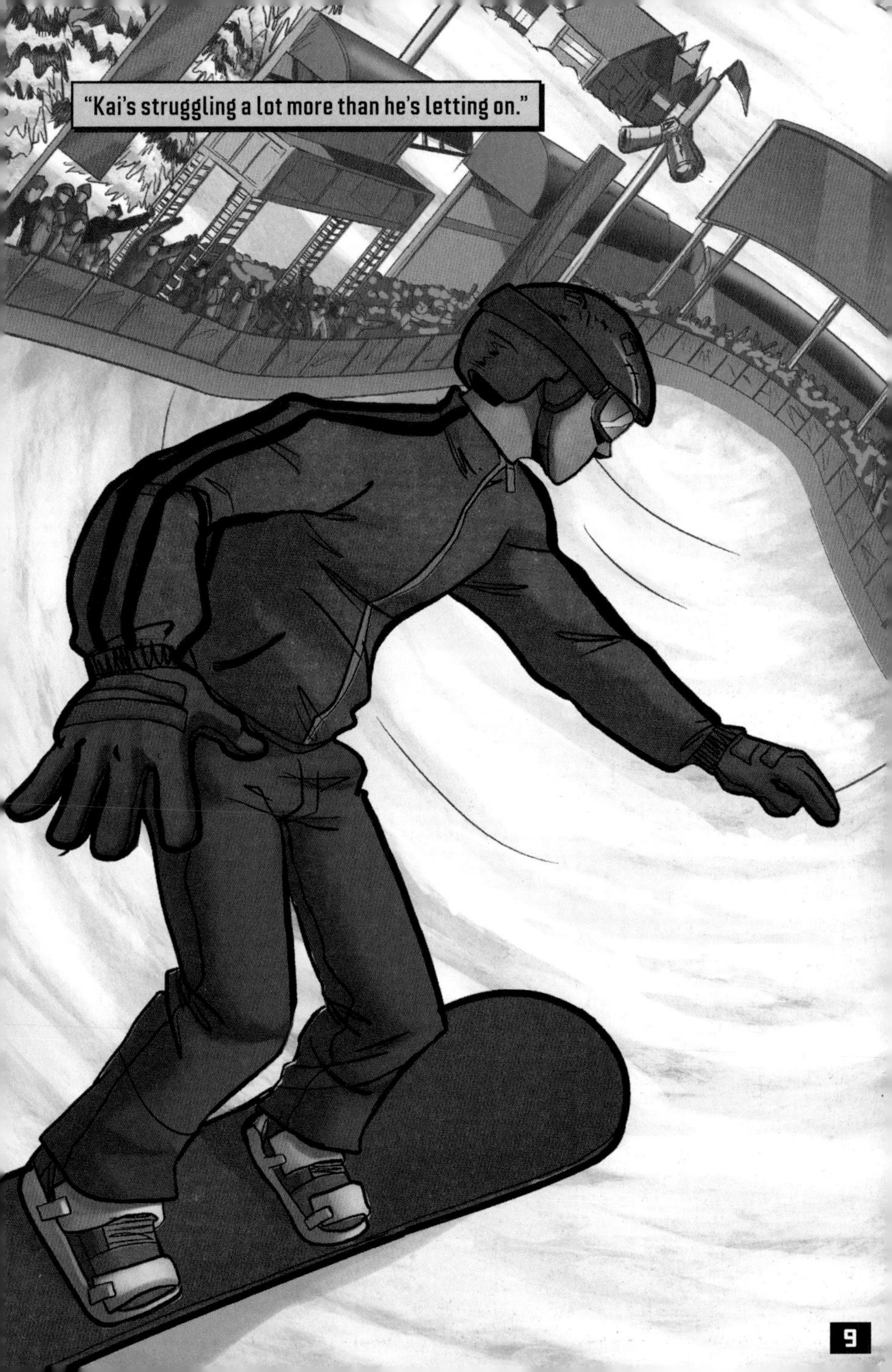
"Kai's struggling a lot more than he's letting on."

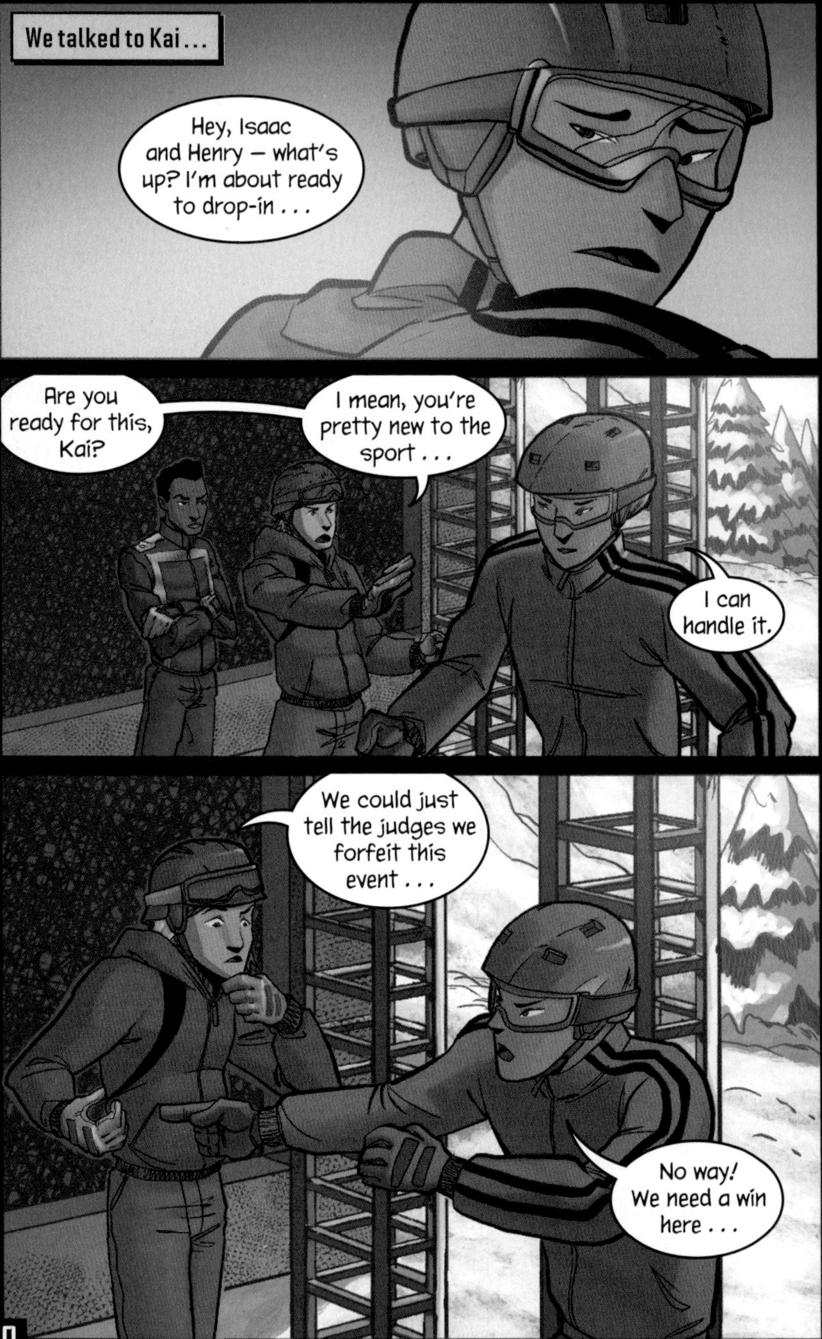
We talked to Kai . . .
Hey, Isaac and Henry — what's up? I'm about ready to drop-in . . .
Are you ready for this, Kai?
I mean, you're pretty new to the sport . . .
I can handle it.
We could just tell the judges we forfeit this event . . .
No way! We need a win here . . .

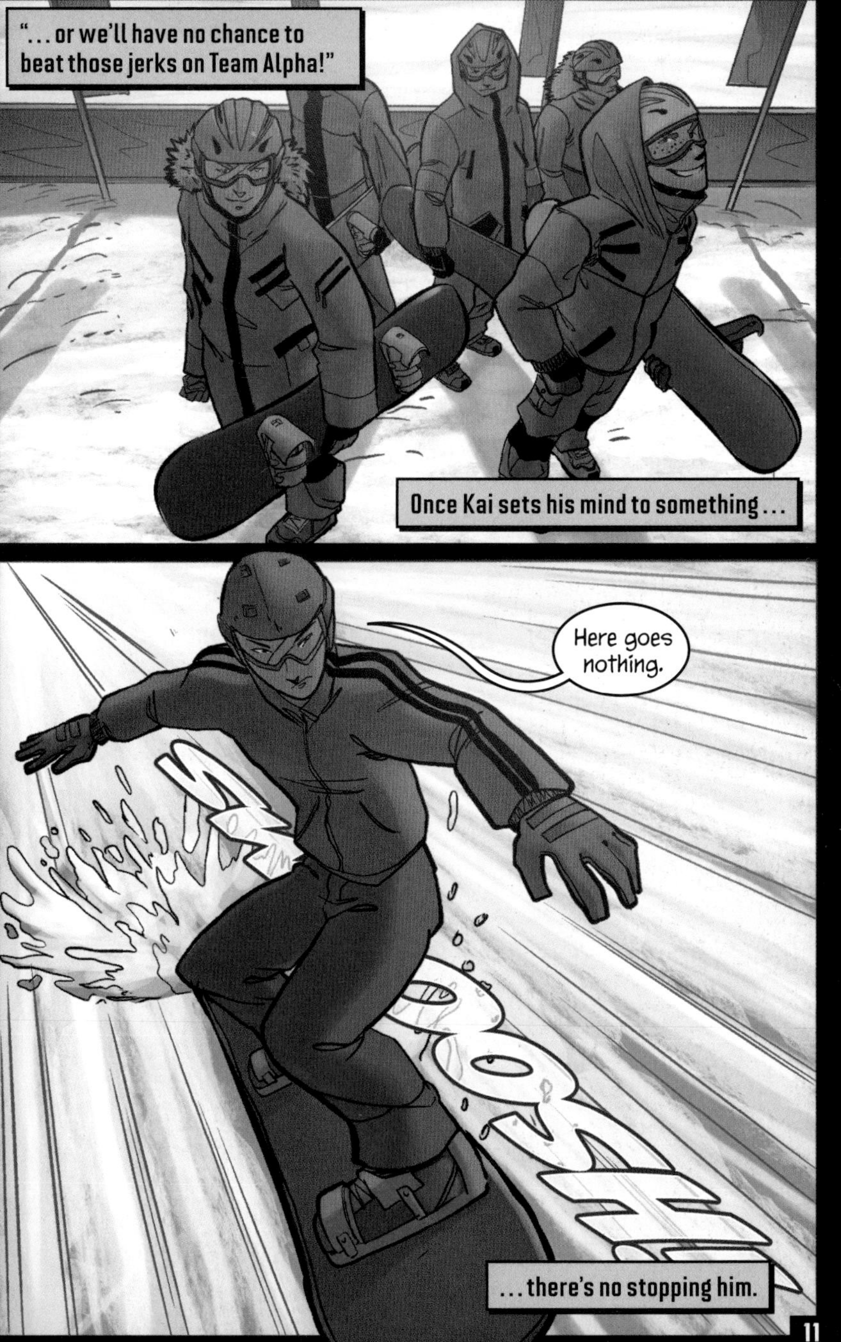
"... or we'll have no chance to beat those jerks on Team Alpha!"
Once Kai sets his mind to something...
Here goes nothing.
... there's no stopping him.

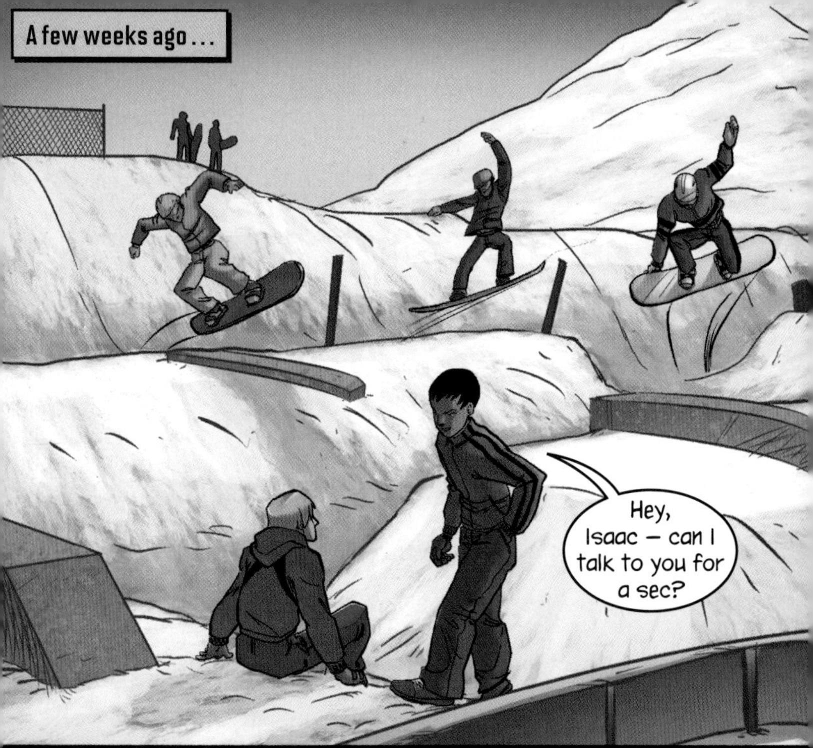
A few weeks ago . . .
Hey, Isaac — can I talk to you for a sec?

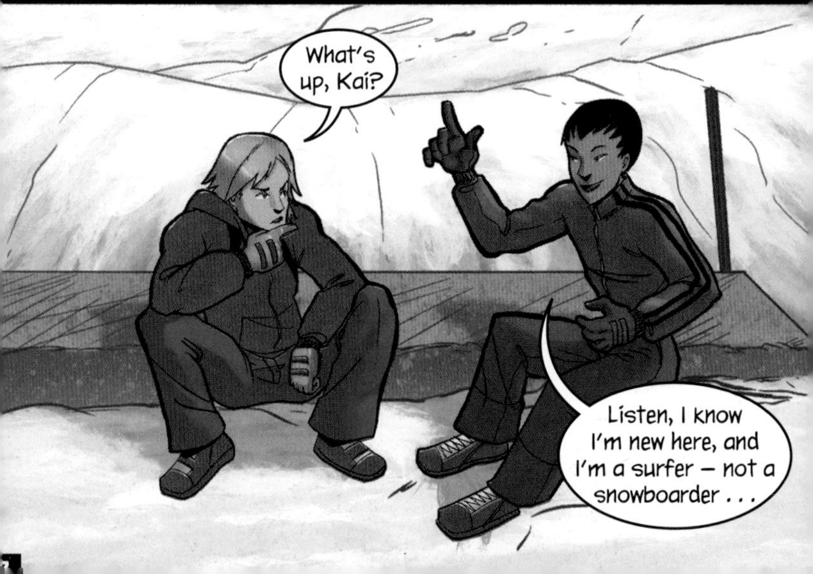
What's up, Kai?
Listen, I know I'm new here, and I'm a surfer — not a snowboarder . . .

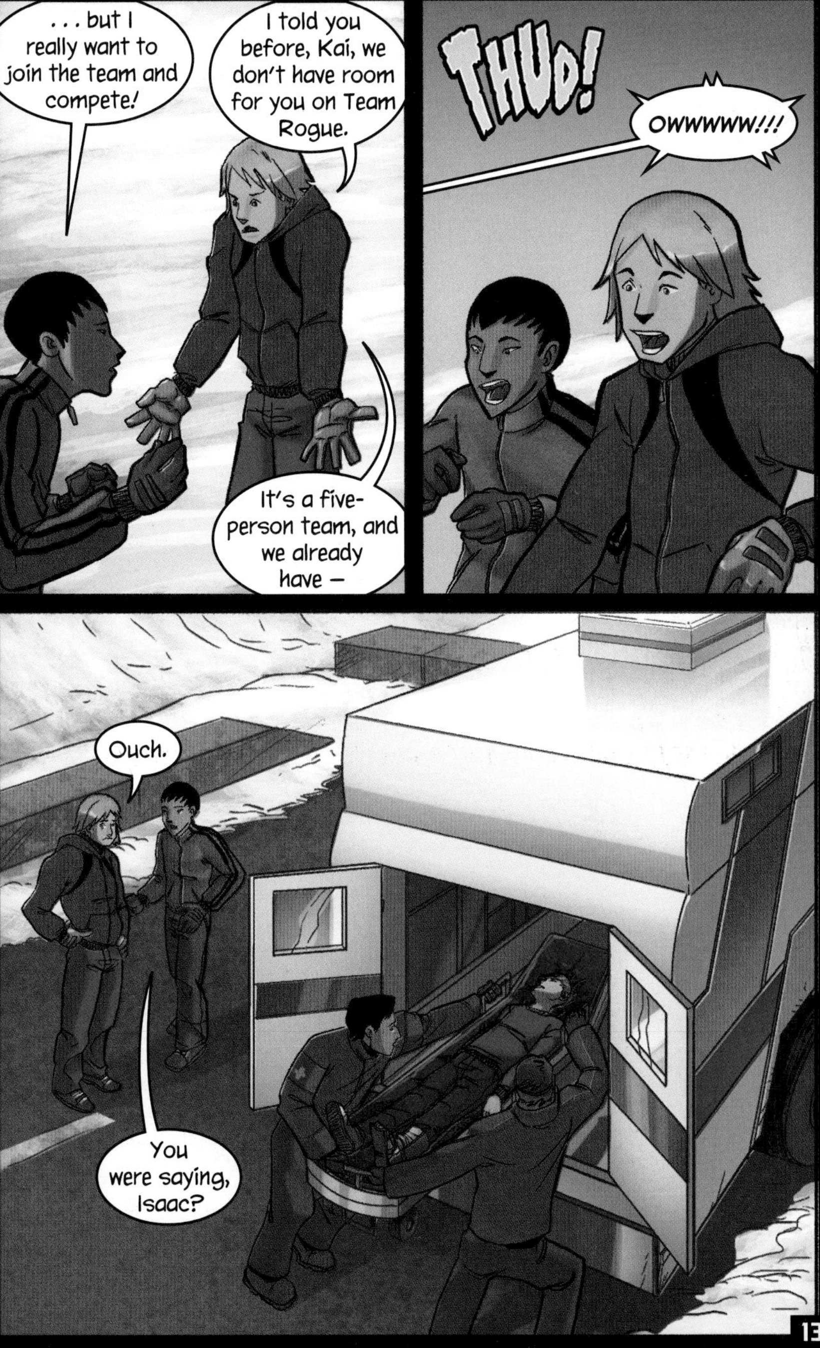
. . . but I really want to join the team and compete!
I told you before, Kai, we don't have room for you on Team Rogue.
It's a five-person team, and we already have —
THUD!
OWWWWW!!!
Ouch.
You were saying, Isaac?

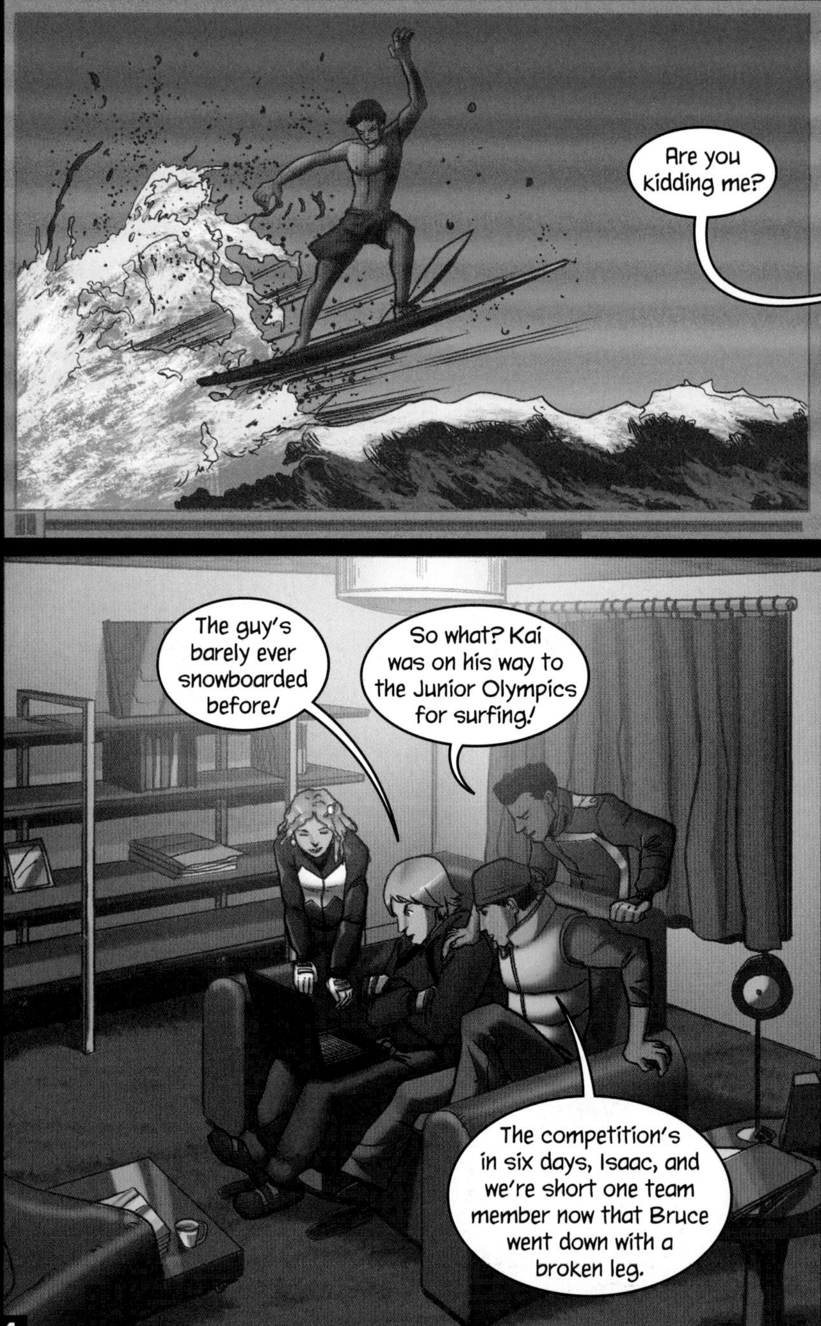
Are you kidding me?
The guy's barely ever snowboarded before!
So what? Kai was on his way to the Junior Olympics for surfing!
The competition's in six days, Isaac, and we're short one team member now that Bruce went down with a broken leg.

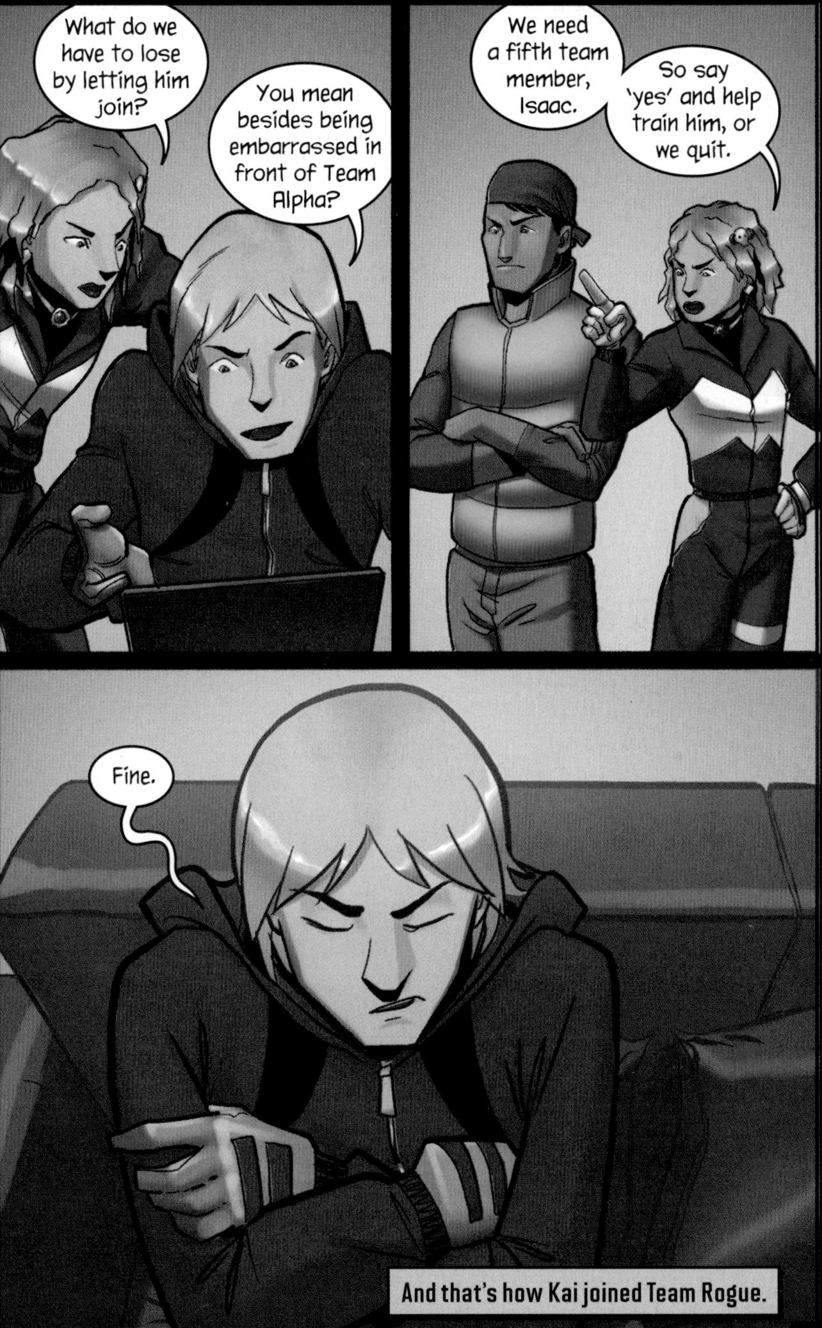
What do we have to lose by letting him join?
You mean besides being embarrassed in front of Team Alpha?
We need a fifth team member, Isaac.
So say 'yes' and help train him, or we quit.
Fine.
And that's how Kai joined Team Rogue.

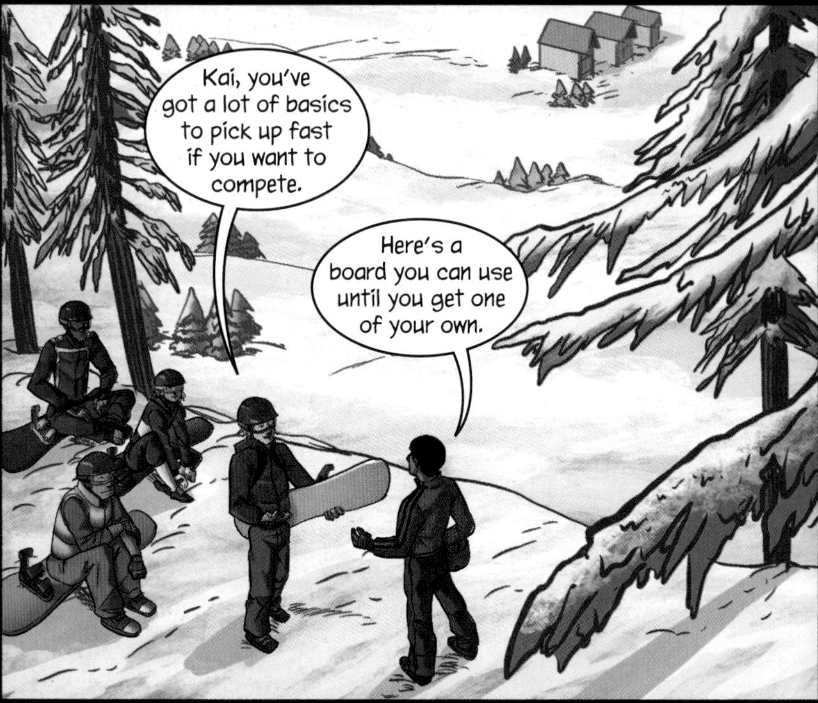
Kai, you've got a lot of basics to pick up fast if you want to compete.
Here's a board you can use until you get one of your own.

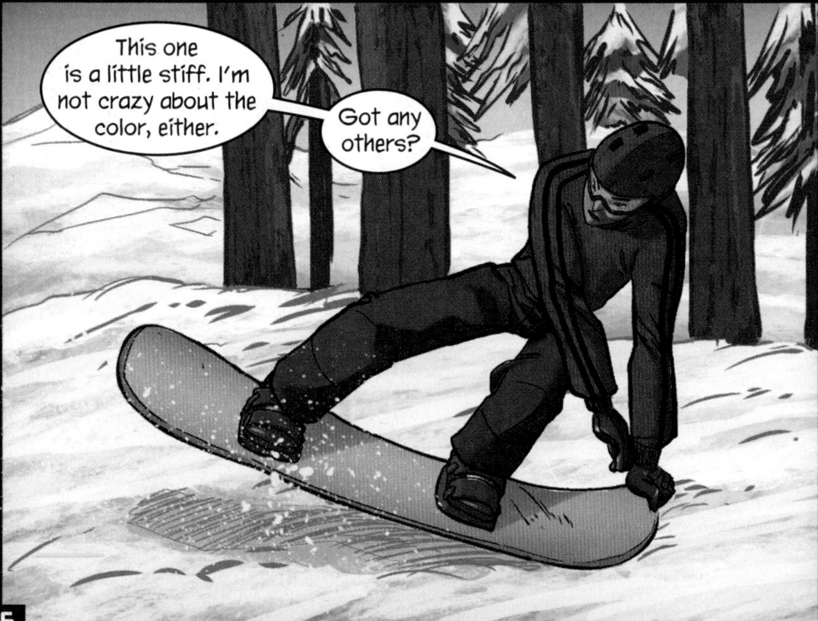
This one is a little stiff. I'm not crazy about the color, either.
Got any others?

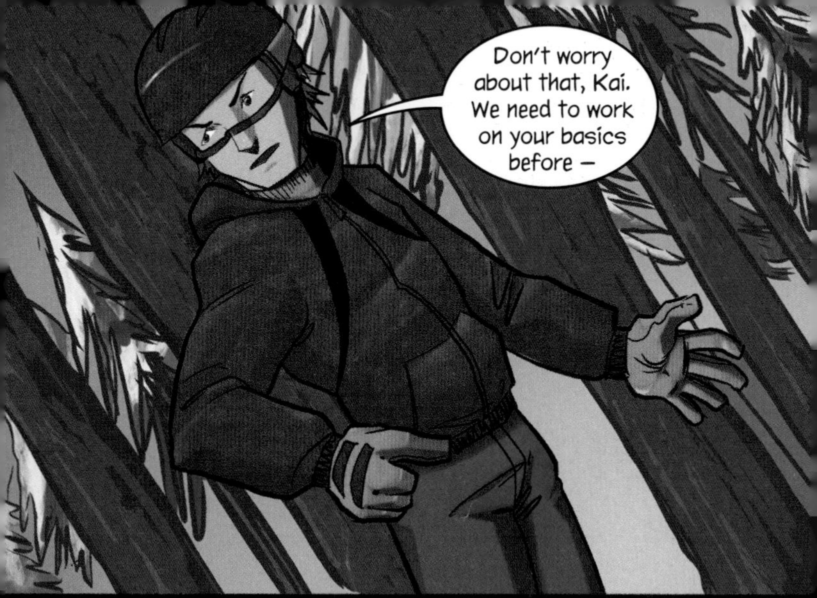
Don't worry about that, Kai. We need to work on your basics before –

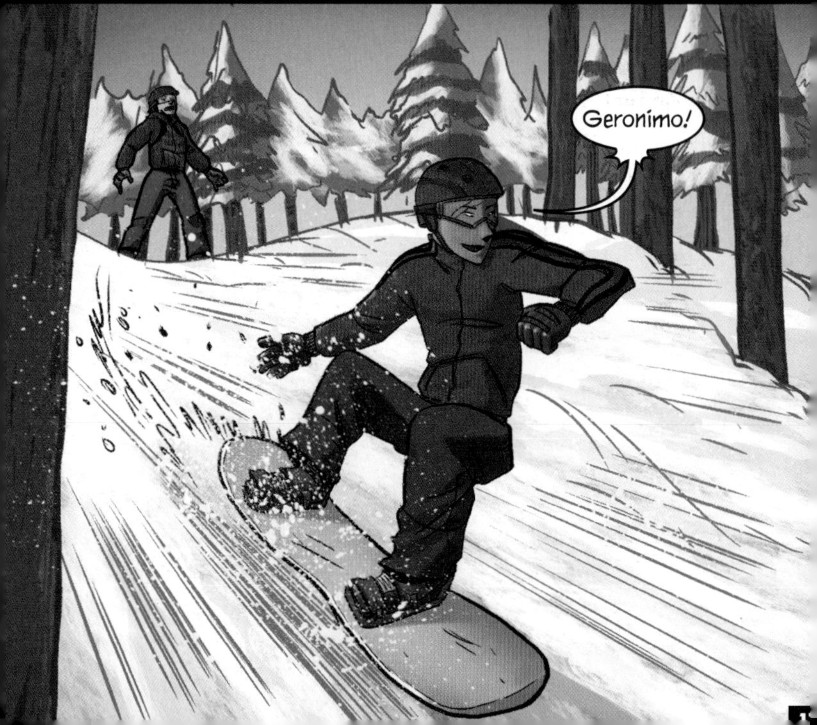
Geronimo!

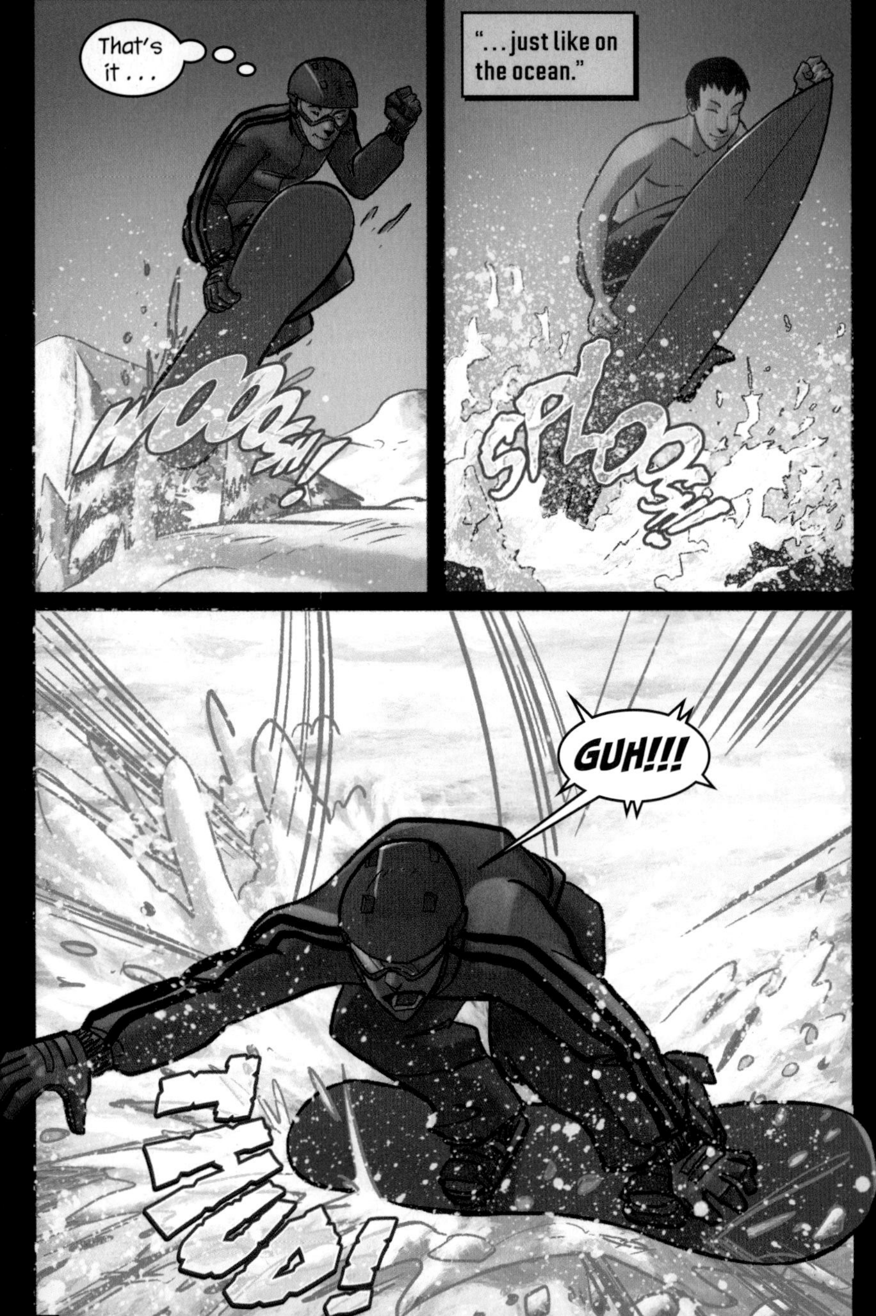
That's it . . .
WOOOSH!!
". . . just like on the ocean."
SPLOOSH!!
GUH!!!
THUD!

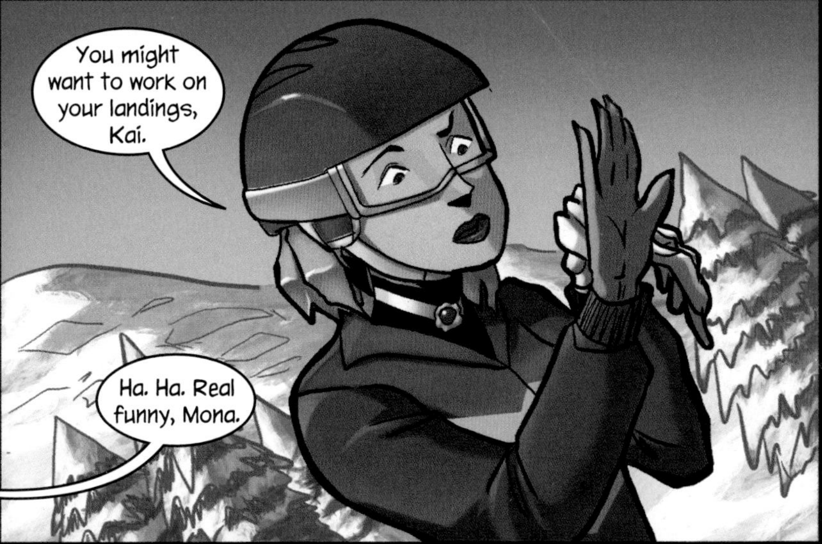
You might want to work on your landings, Kai.
Ha. Ha. Real funny, Mona.

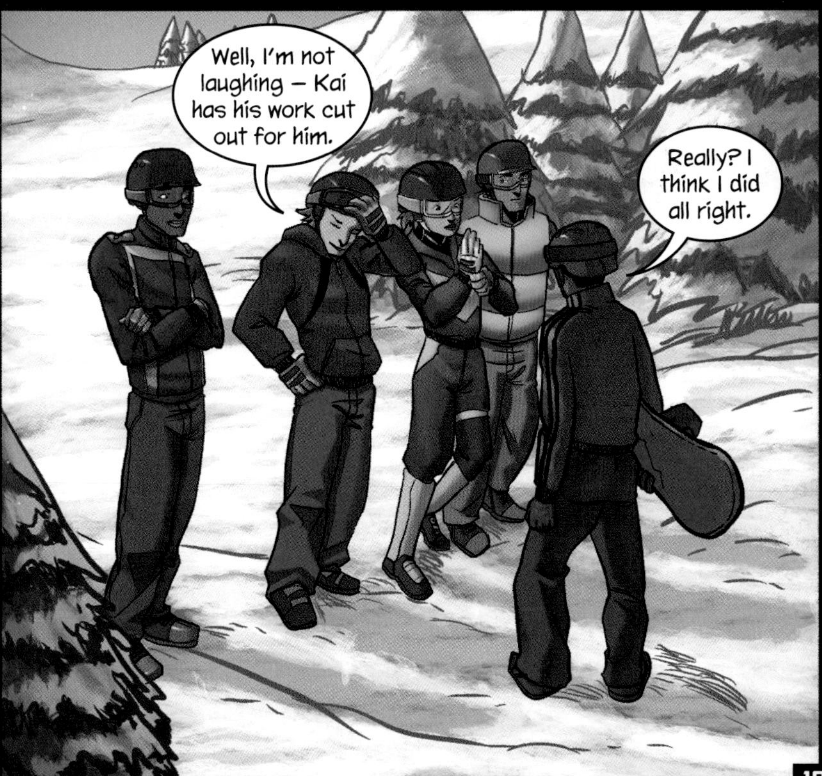
Well, I'm not laughing — Kai has his work cut out for him.
Really? I think I did all right.

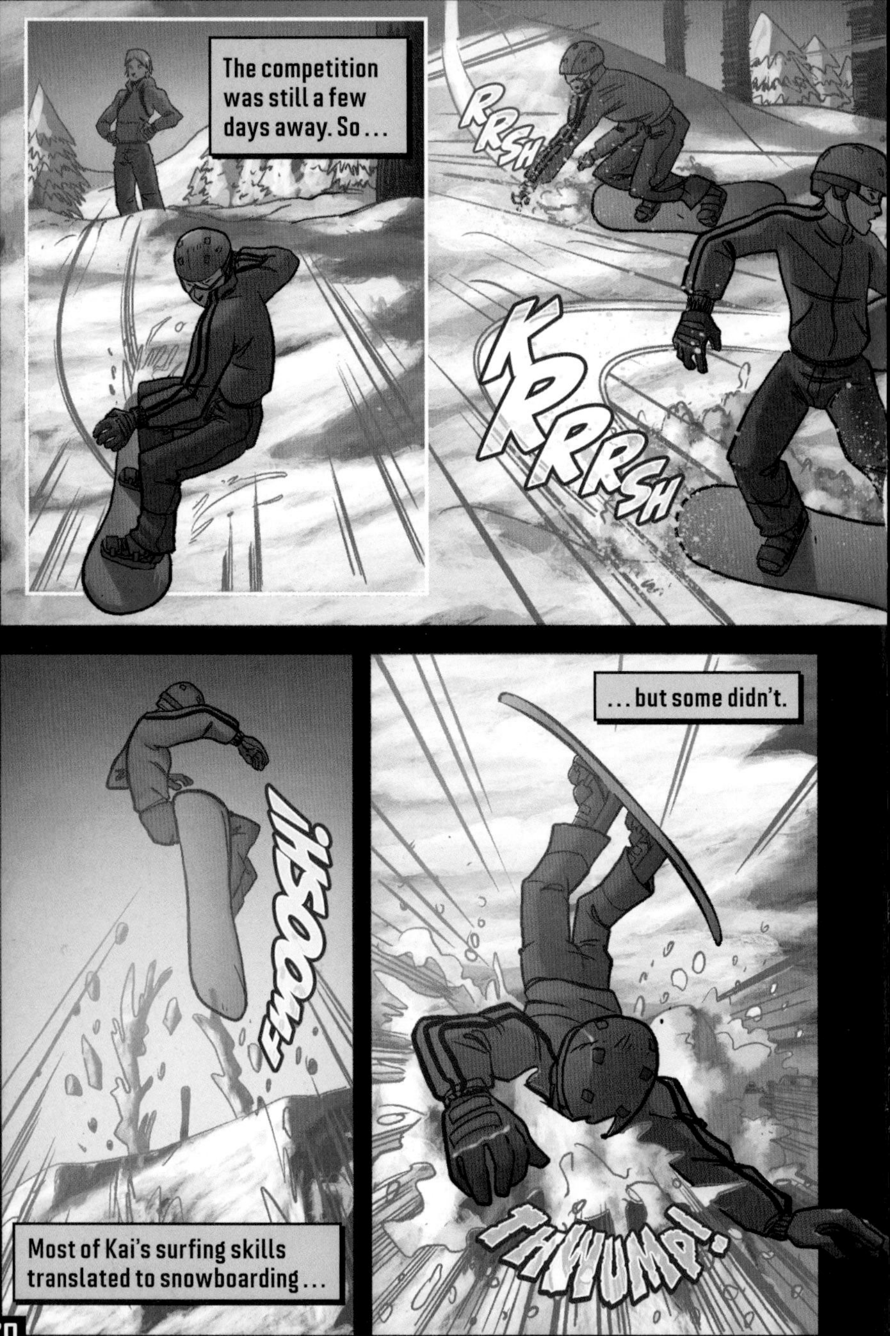
The competition was still a few days away. So . . .
RRSH
KRRRSH
FWOOSH!
Most of Kai's surfing skills translated to snowboarding . . .
. . . but some didn't.
THWUMP!

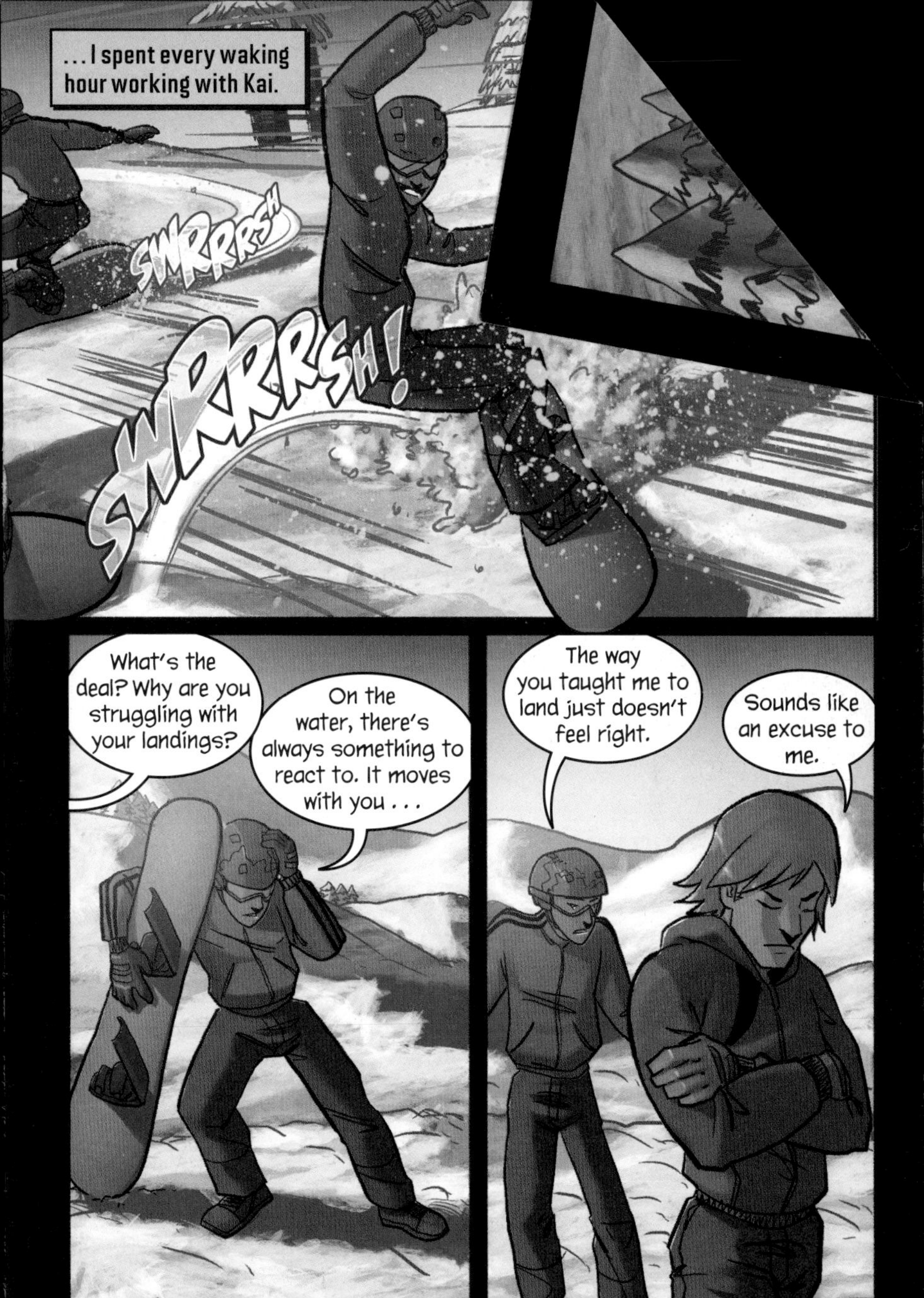

. . . I spent every waking hour working with Kai.
SWRRRSH
SWRRRSH!
What's the deal? Why are you struggling with your landings?
On the water, there's always something to react to. It moves with you . . .
The way you taught me to land just doesn't feel right.
Sounds like an excuse to me.

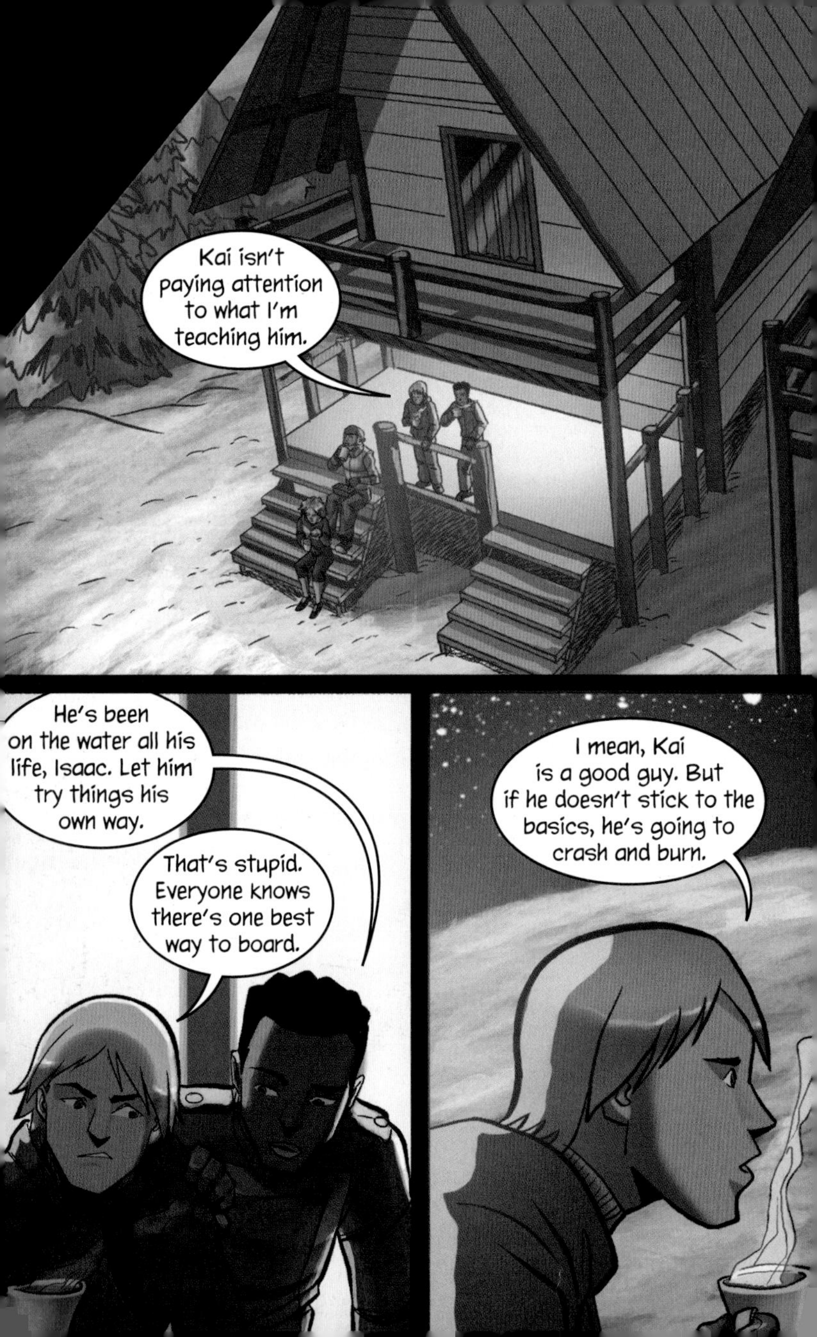
Kai isn't paying attention to what I'm teaching him.
He's been on the water all his life, Isaac. Let him try things his own way.
That's stupid. Everyone knows there's one best way to board.
I mean, Kai is a good guy. But if he doesn't stick to the basics, he's going to crash and burn.

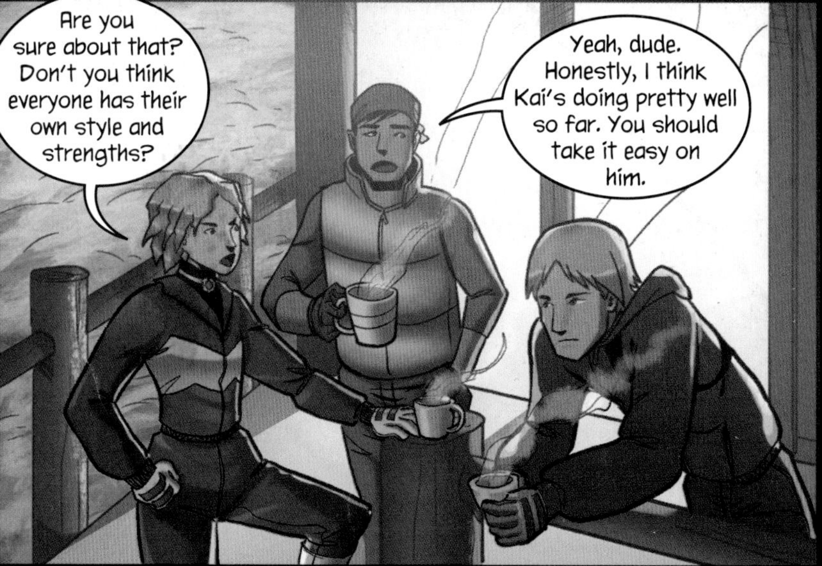
Are you sure about that? Don't you think everyone has their own style and strengths?
Yeah, dude. Honestly, I think Kai's doing pretty well so far. You should take it easy on him.

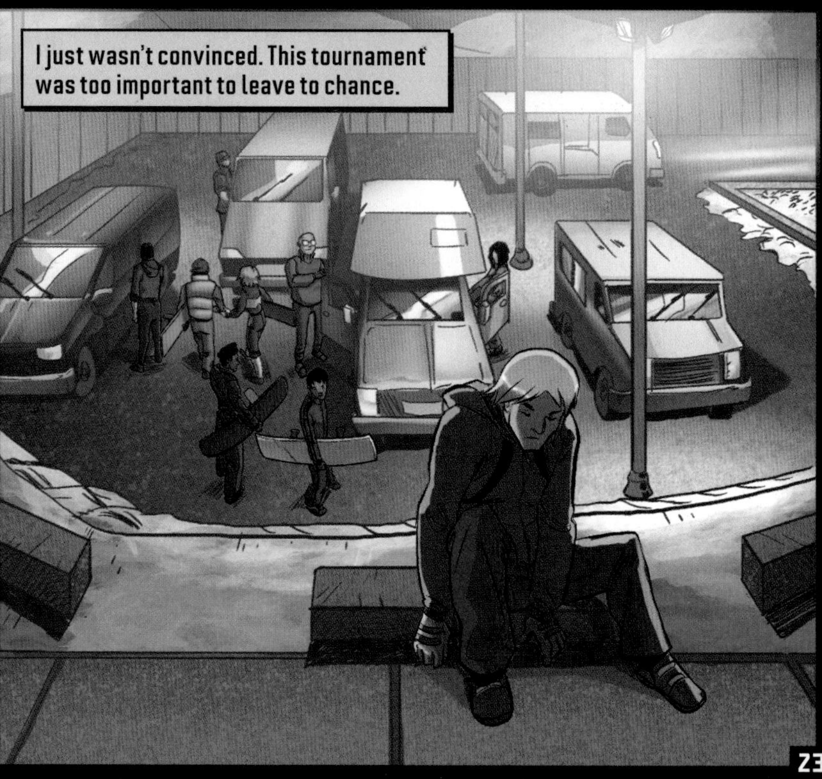
I just wasn't convinced. This tournament was too important to leave to chance.

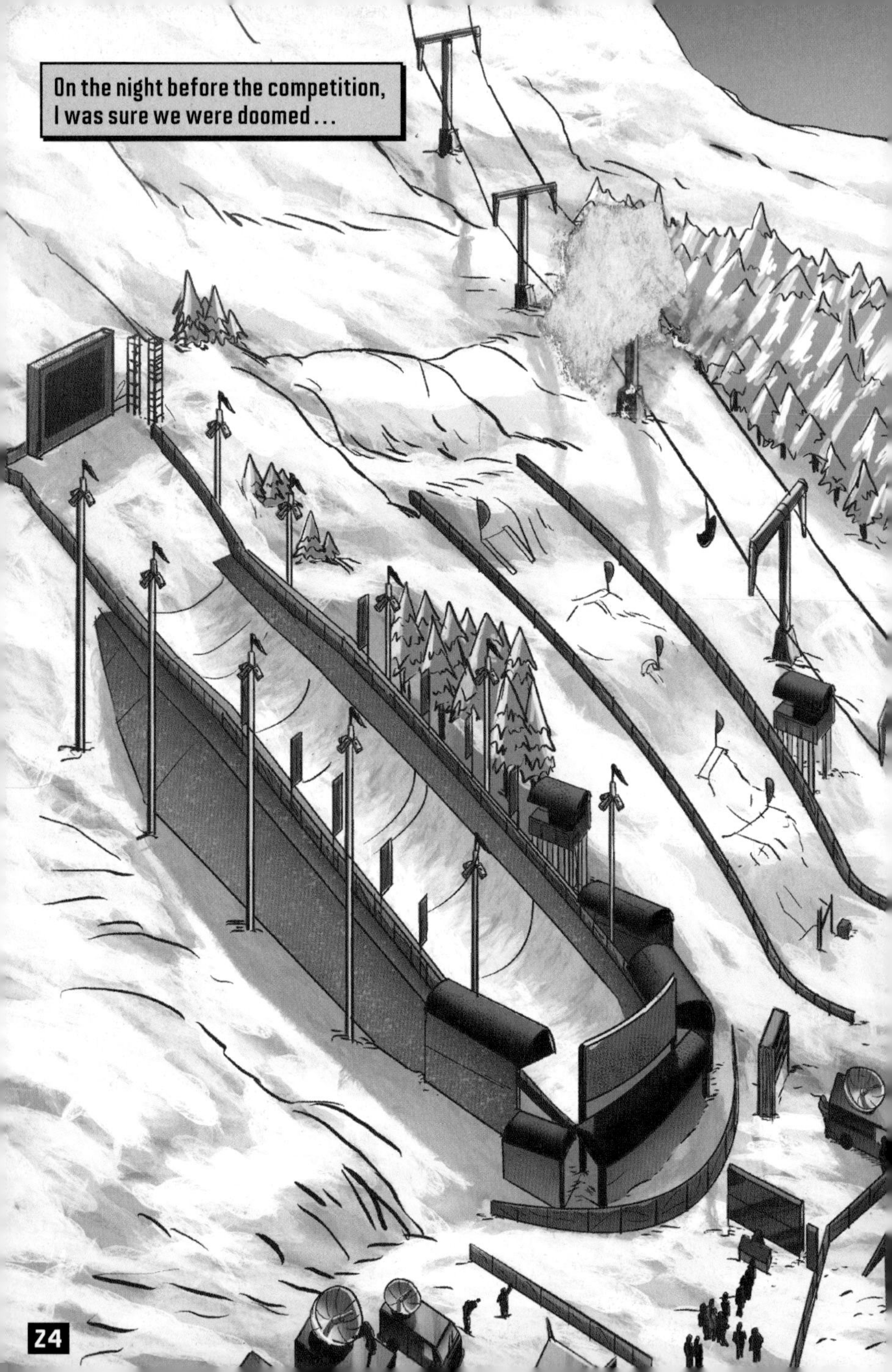
On the night before the competition, I was sure we were doomed . . .

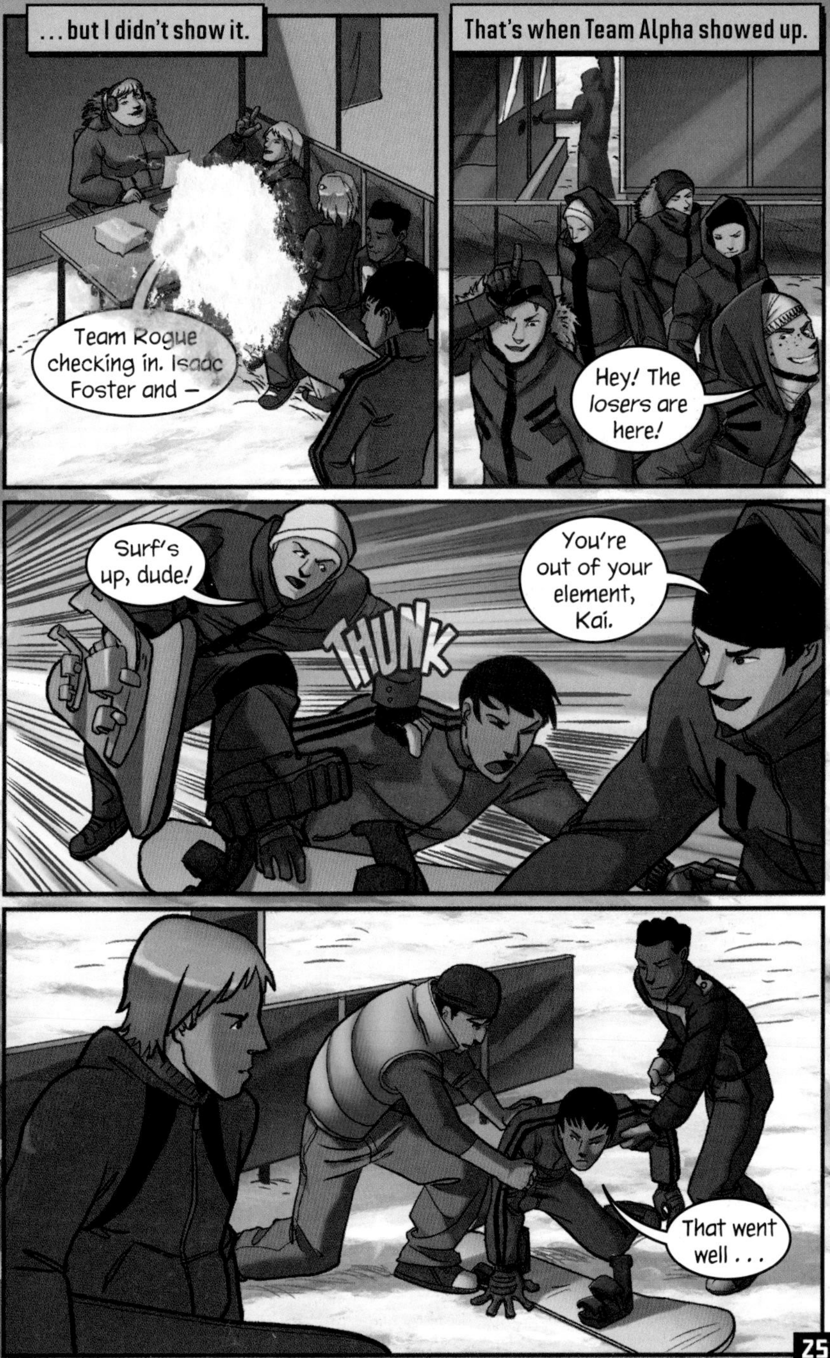
. . . but I didn't show it.
Team Rogue checking in. Isaac Foster and —
That's when Team Alpha showed up.
Hey! The losers are here!
Surf's up, dude!
THUNK
You're out of your element, Kai.
That went well . . .

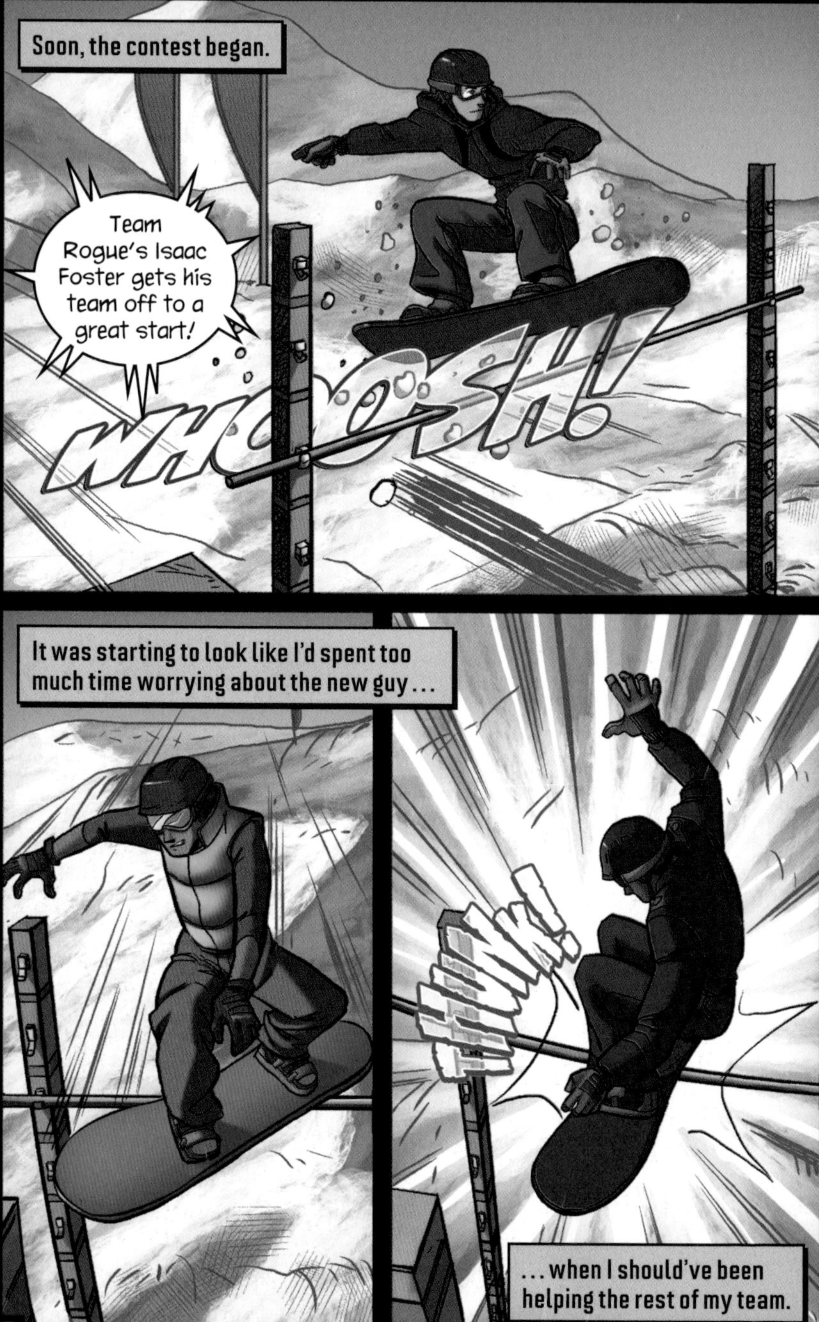
Soon, the contest began.
Team Rogue's Isaac Foster gets his team off to a great start!
WHOOSH!
It was starting to look like I'd spent too much time worrying about the new guy . . .
. . . when I should've been helping the rest of my team.

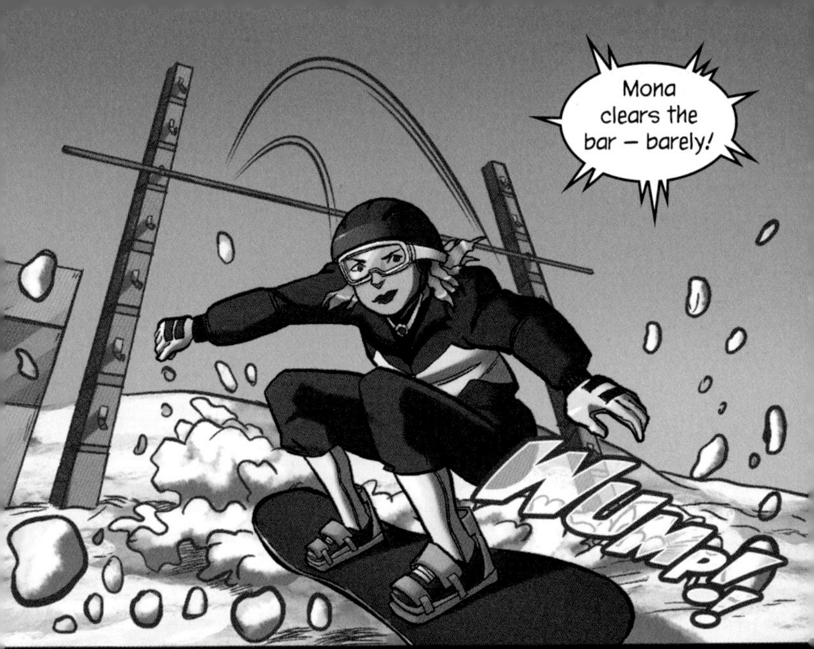

Mona clears the bar — barely!
WUMP!

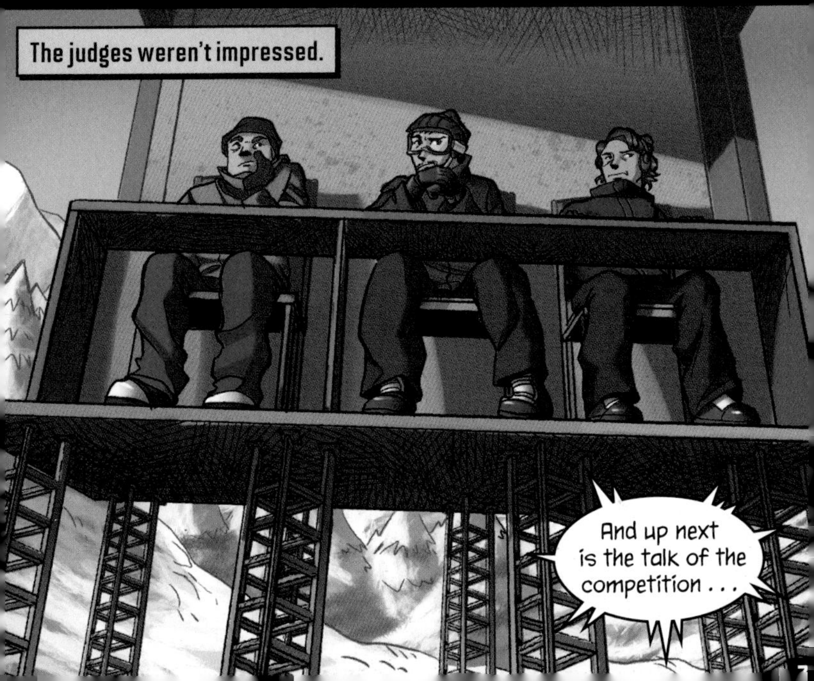

The judges weren't impressed.
And up next is the talk of the competition . . .

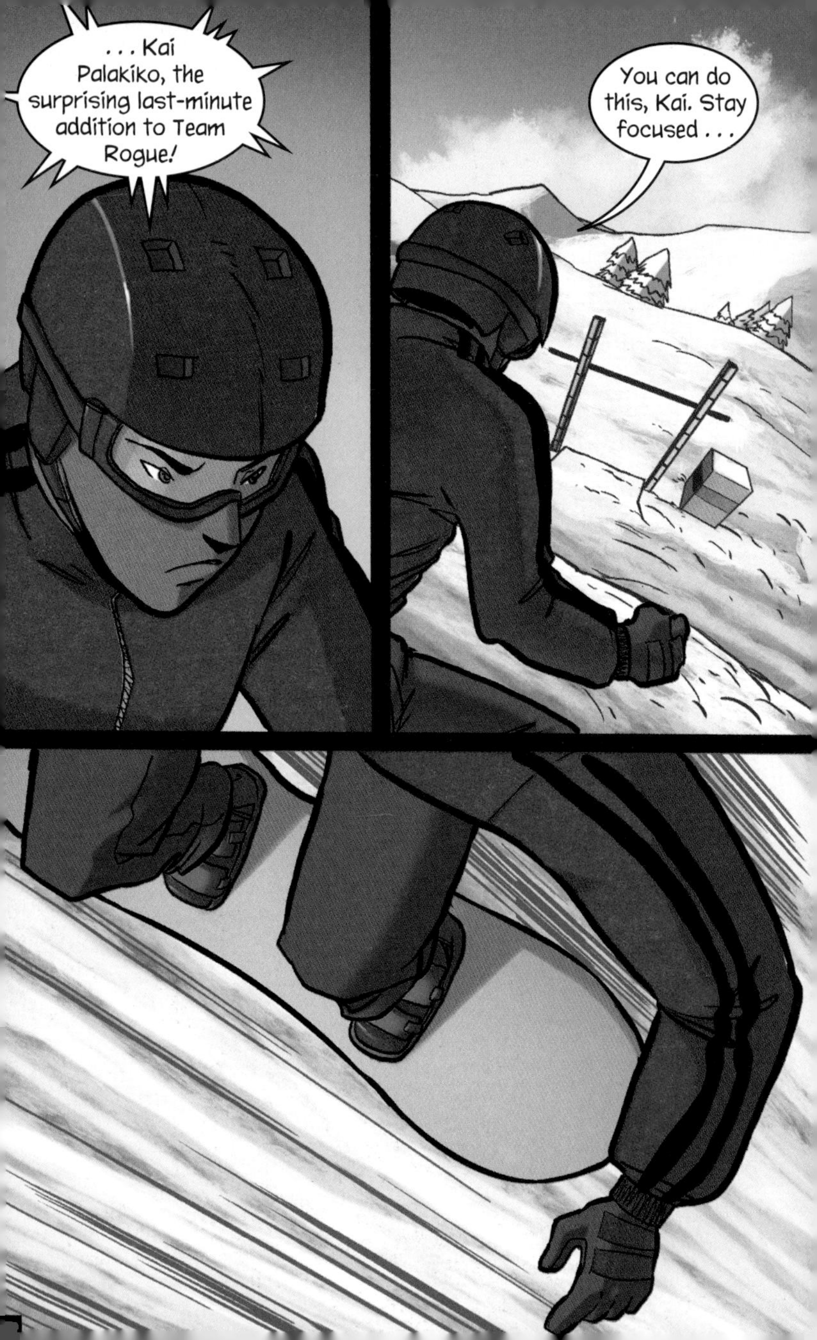
. . . Kai Palakiko, the surprising last-minute addition to Team Rogue!
You can do this, Kai. Stay focused . . .

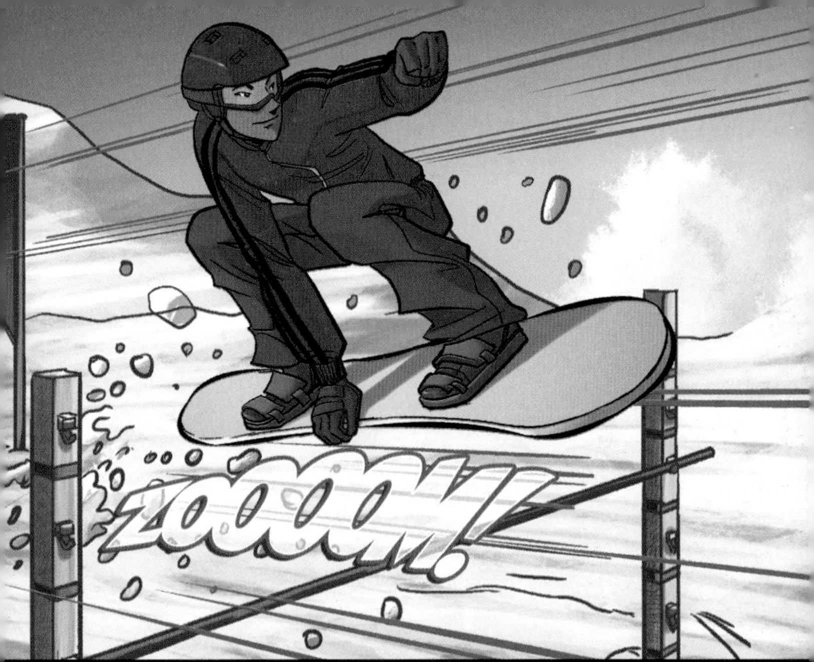
ZOOOM!

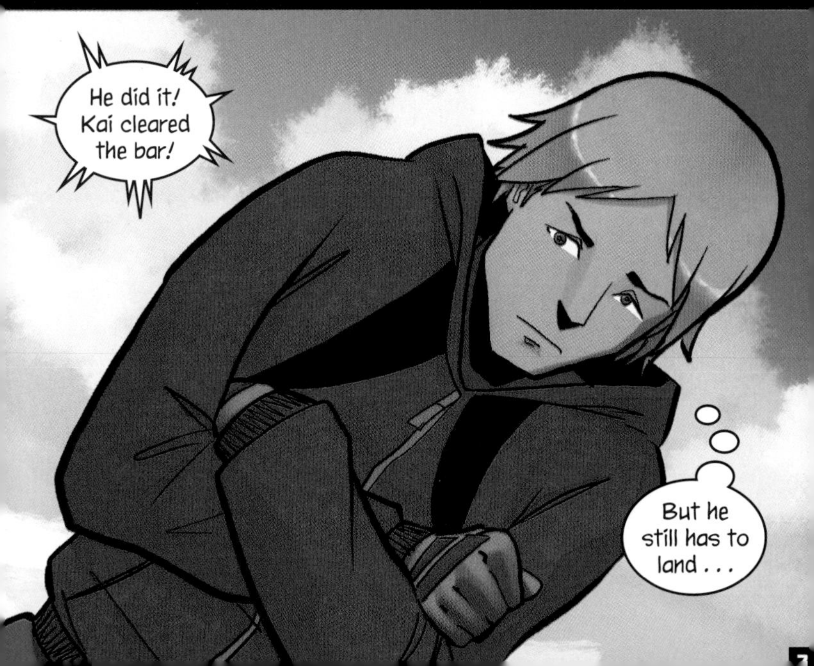
He did it! Kai cleared the bar!
But he still has to land . . .

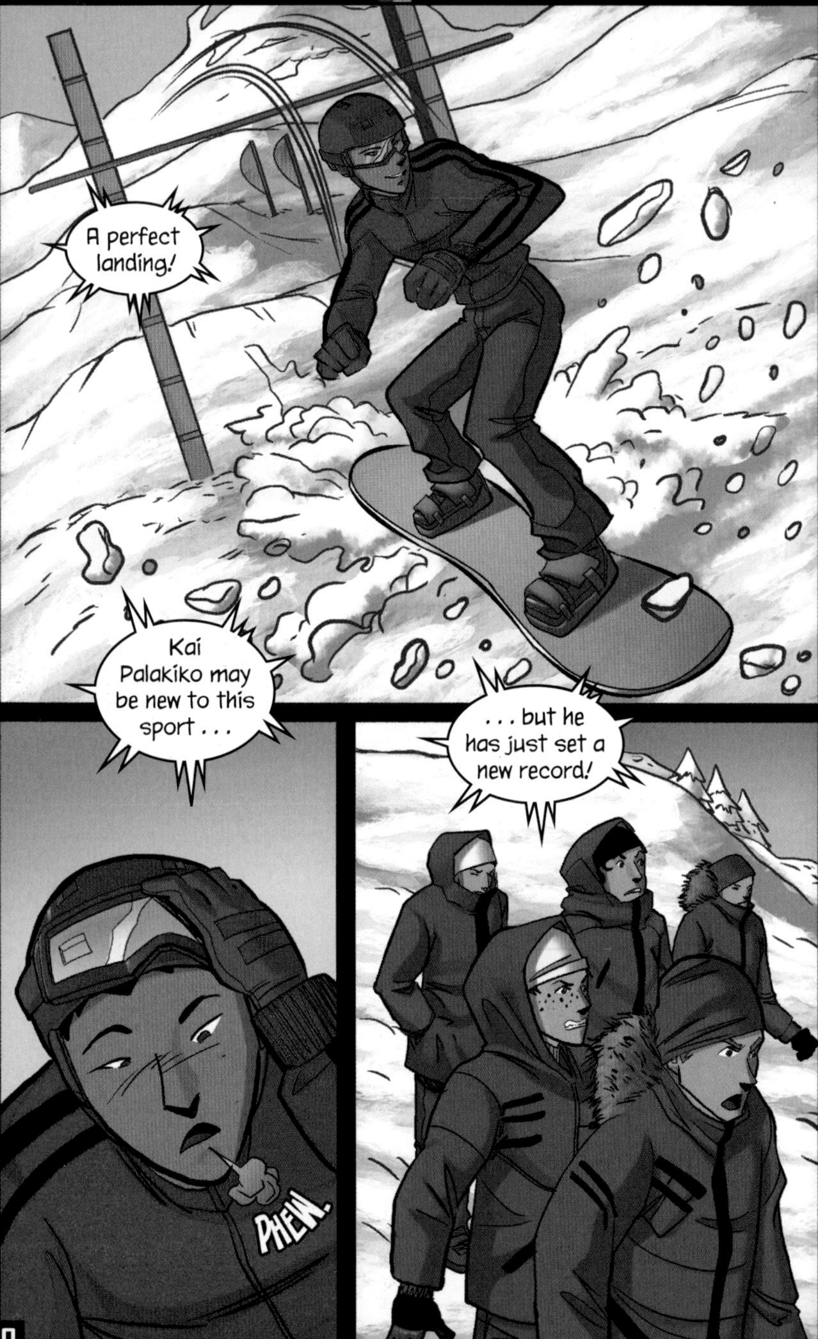
A perfect landing!
Kai Palakiko may be new to this sport . . .
. . . but he has just set a new record!
PHEW.

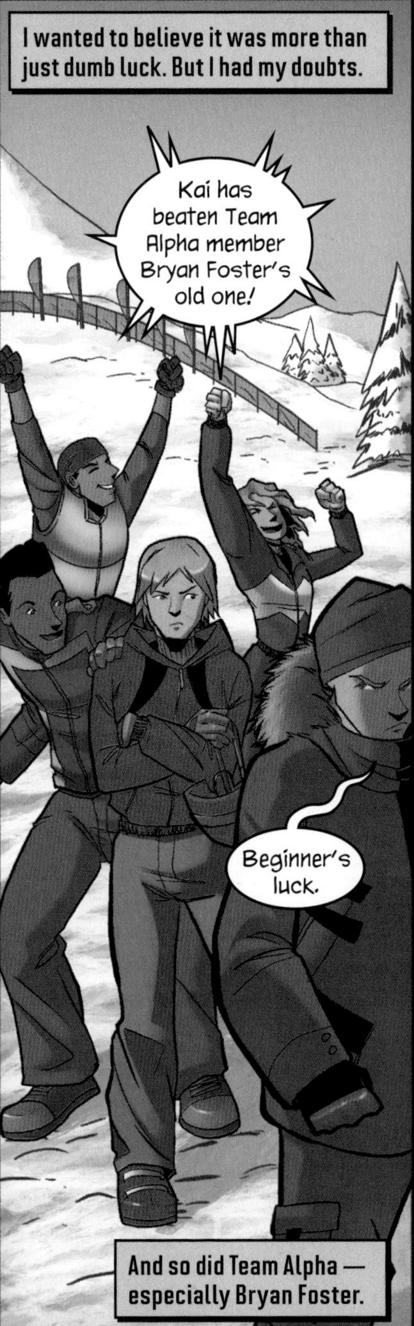
I wanted to believe it was more than just dumb luck. But I had my doubts.
Kai has beaten Team Alpha member Bryan Foster's old one!
Beginner's luck.
And so did Team Alpha — especially Bryan Foster.

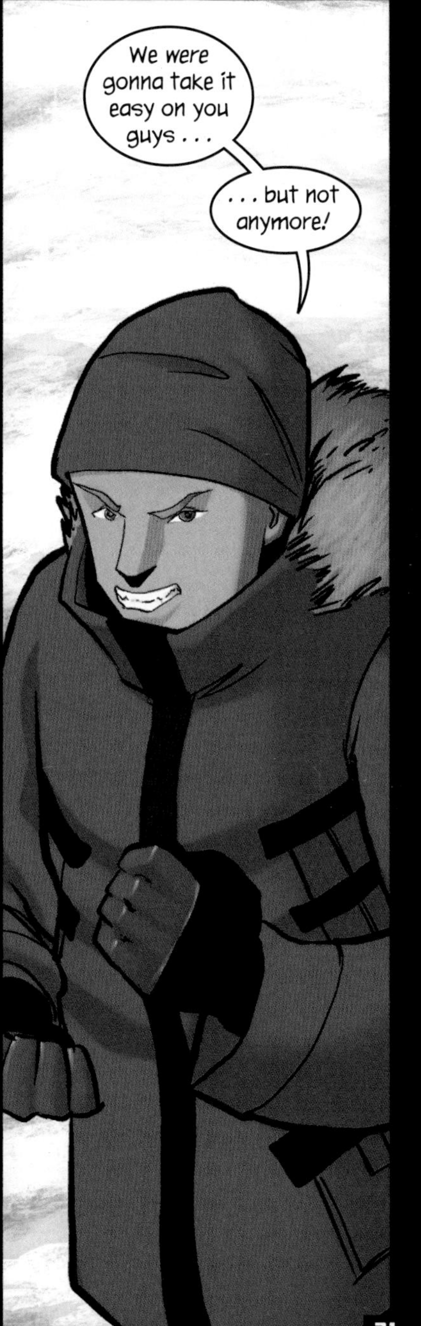
We were gonna take it easy on you guys . . .
. . . but not anymore!

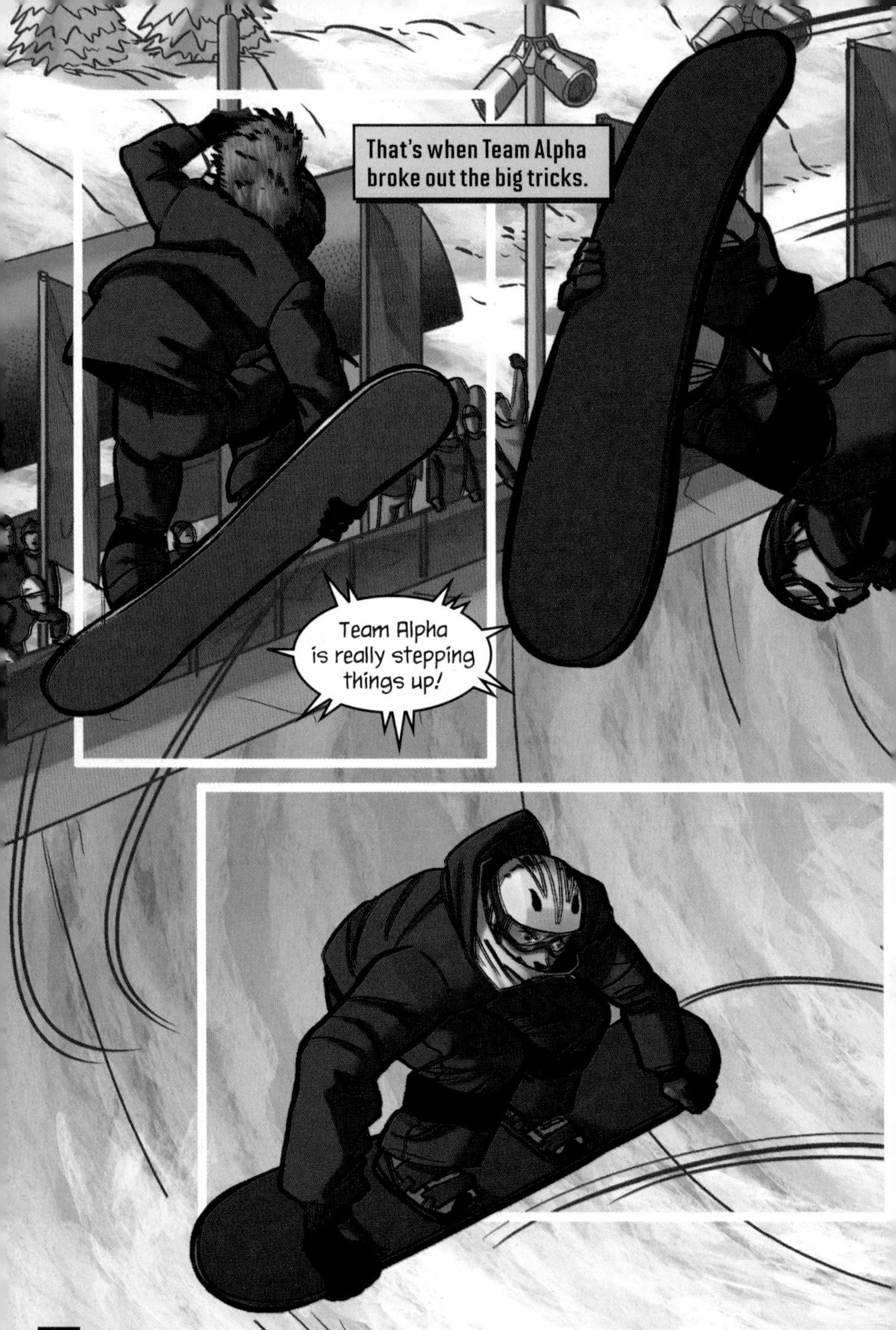
That's when Team Alpha broke out the big tricks.
Team Alpha is really stepping things up!

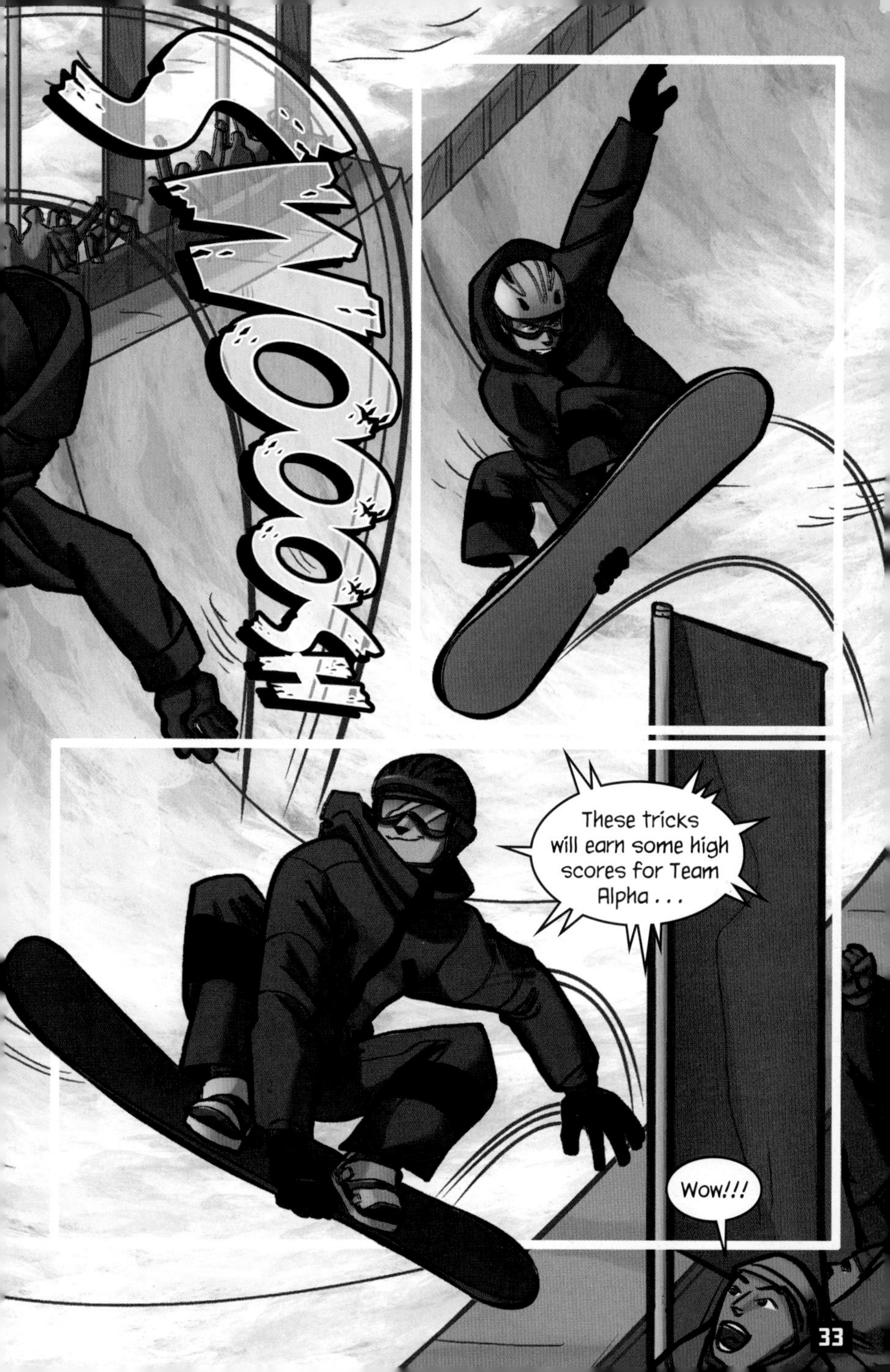
WHOOSH!
These tricks will earn some high scores for Team Alpha . . .
Wow!!!

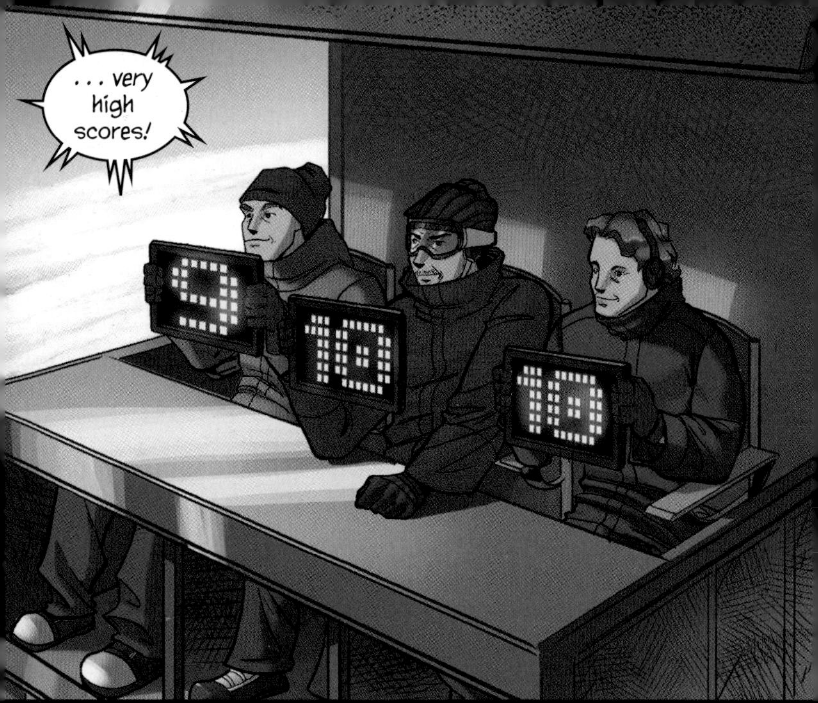
. . . very high scores!
9
10
10

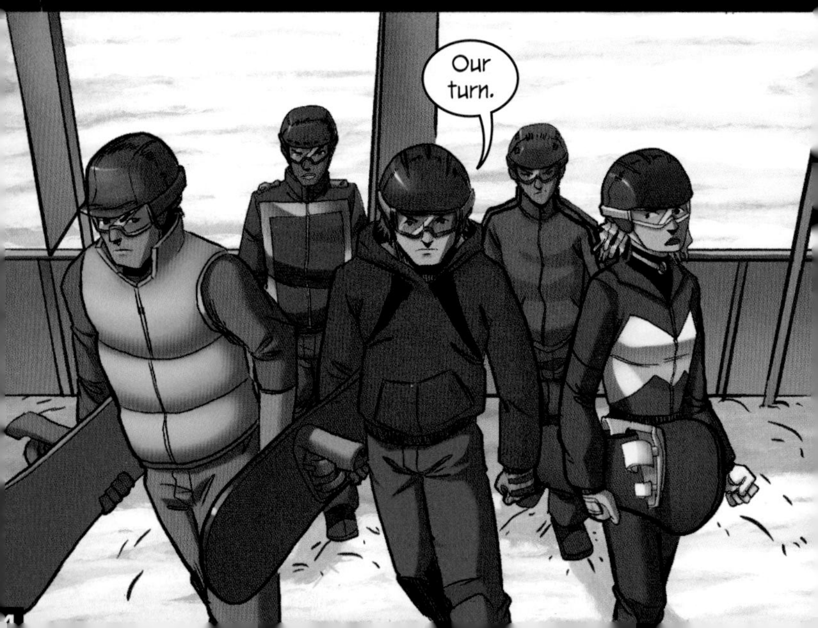
Our turn.

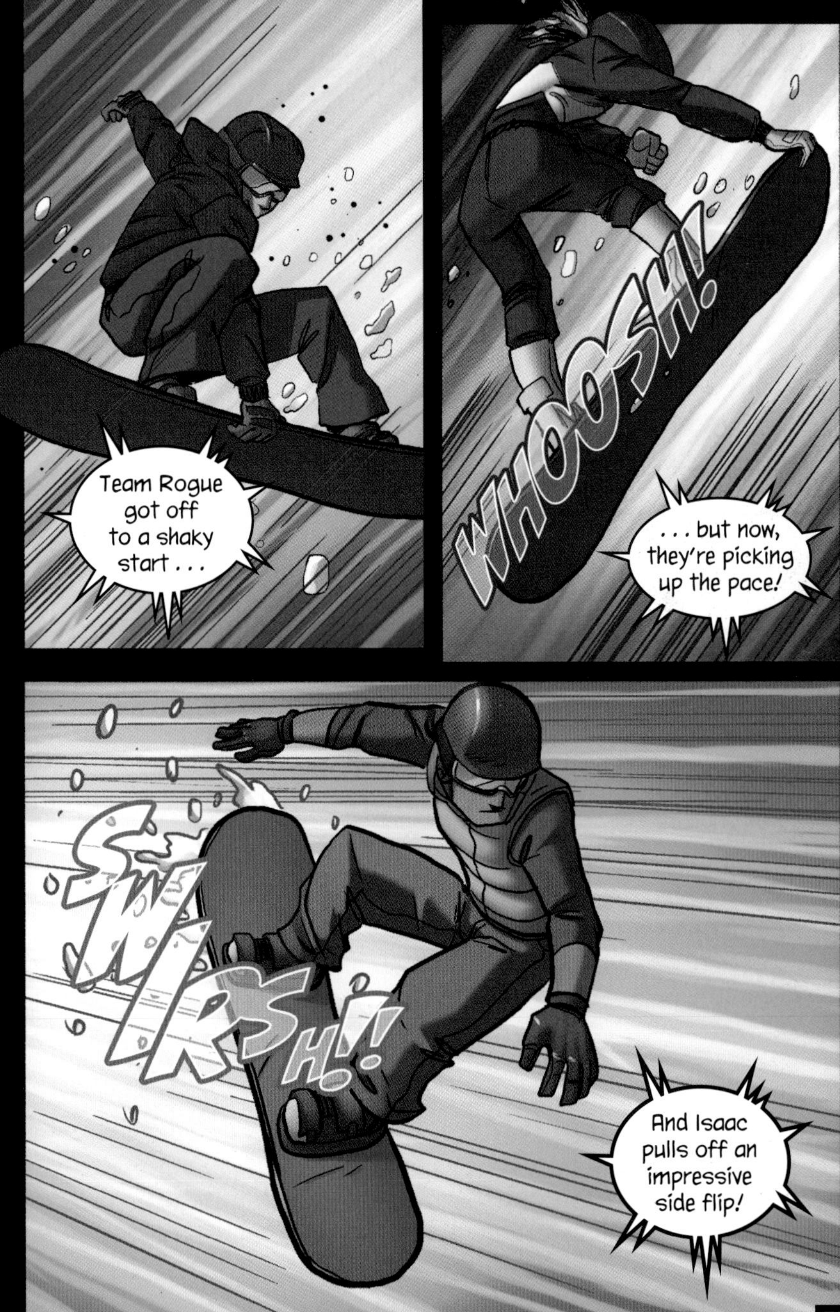
Team Rogue got off to a shaky start . . .
WHOOSH!
. . . but now, they're picking up the pace!
SWRSH!!
And Isaac pulls off an impressive side flip!

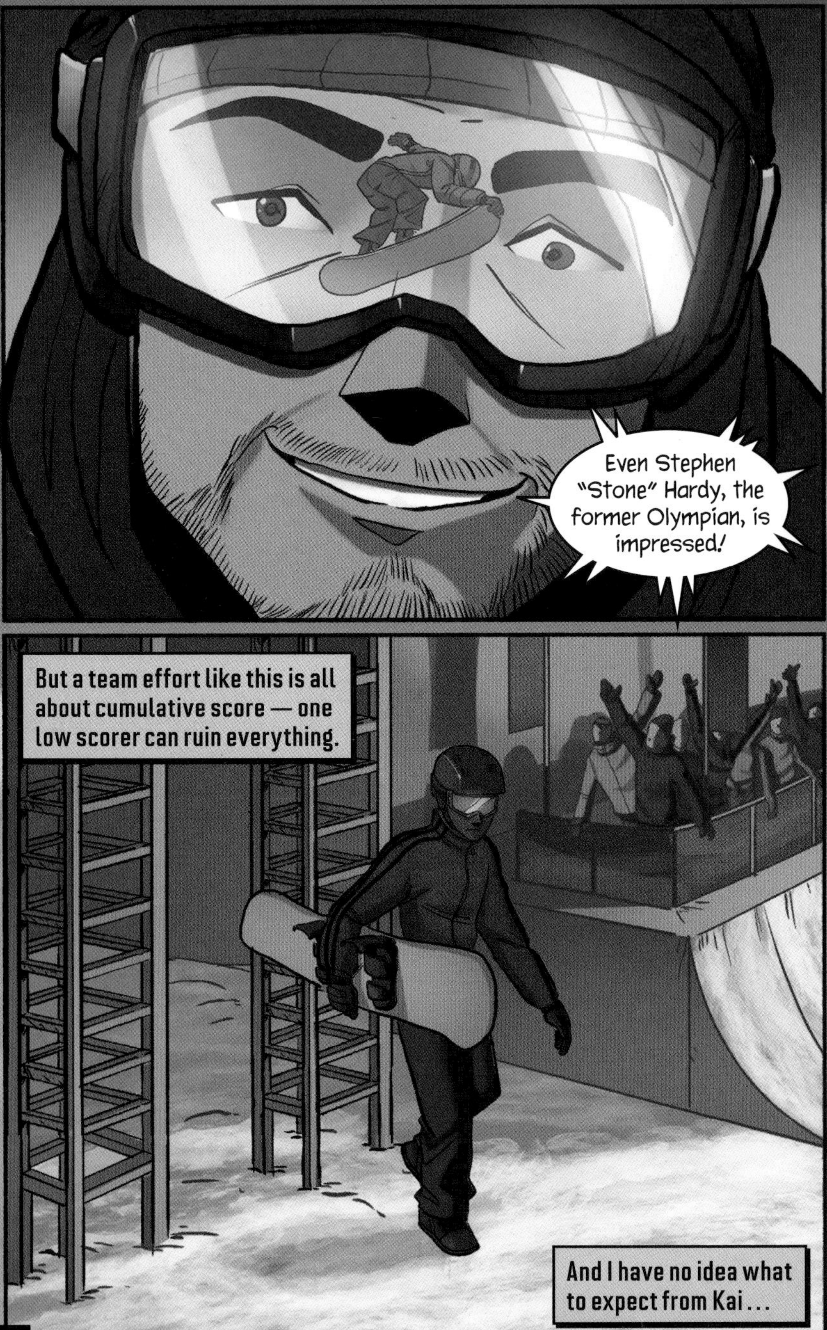
Even Stephen "Stone" Hardy, the former Olympian, is impressed!
But a team effort like this is all about cumulative score — one low scorer can ruin everything.
And I have no idea what to expect from Kai . . .

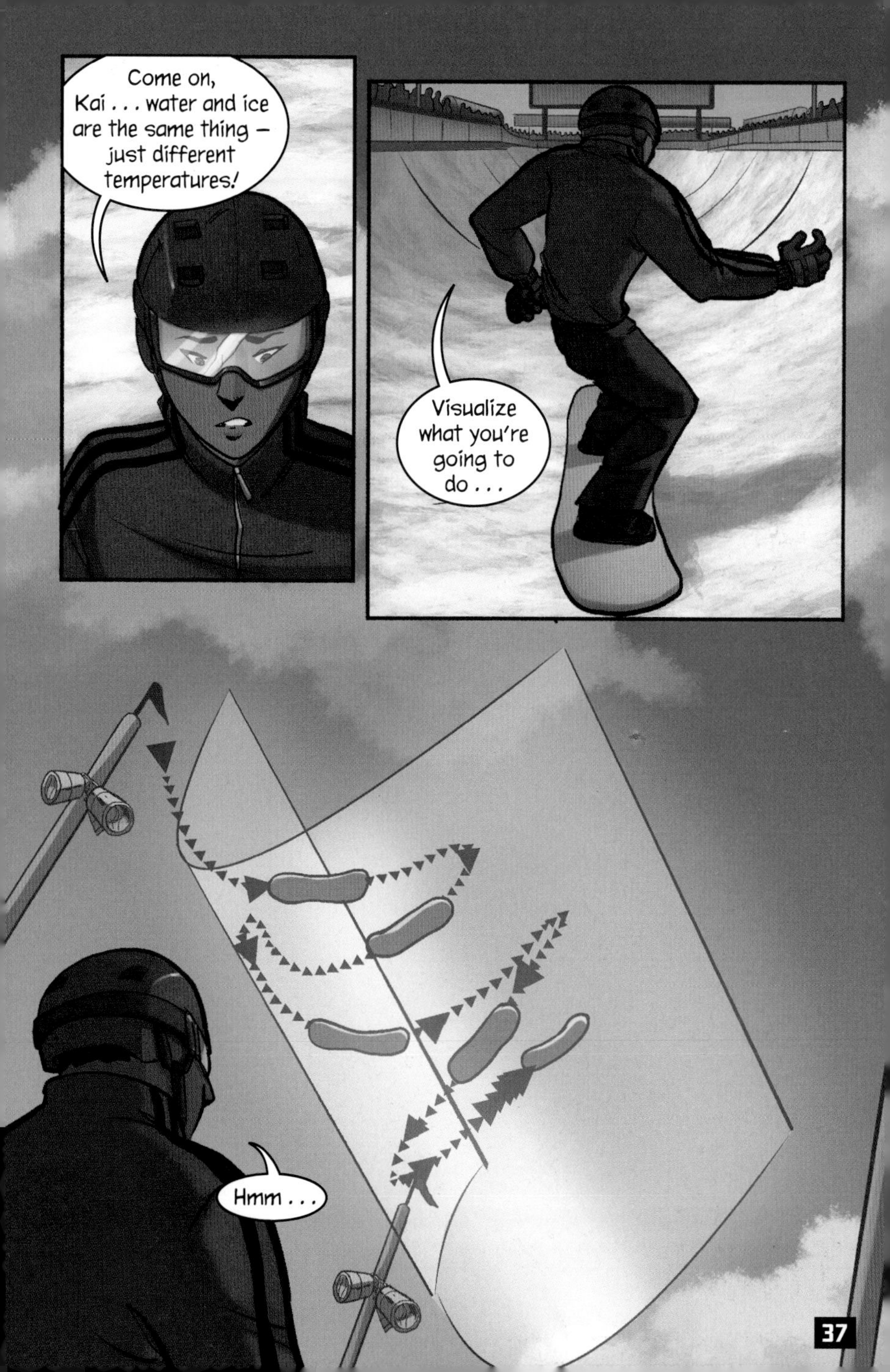

Come on, Kai . . . water and ice are the same thing — just different temperatures!
Visualize what you're going to do . . .
Hmm . . .

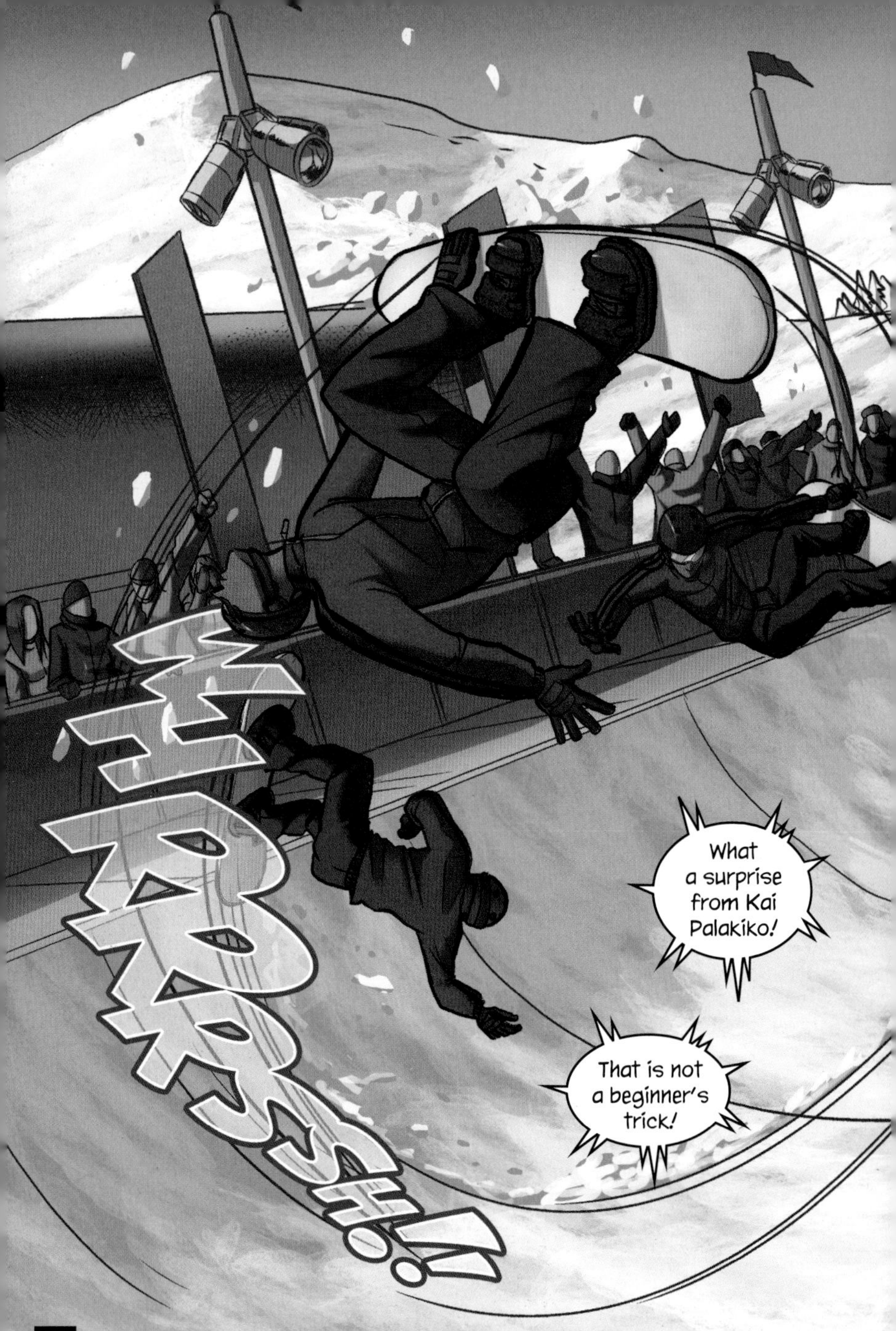
WHRRSSH!!
What a surprise from Kai Palakiko!
That is not a beginner's trick!

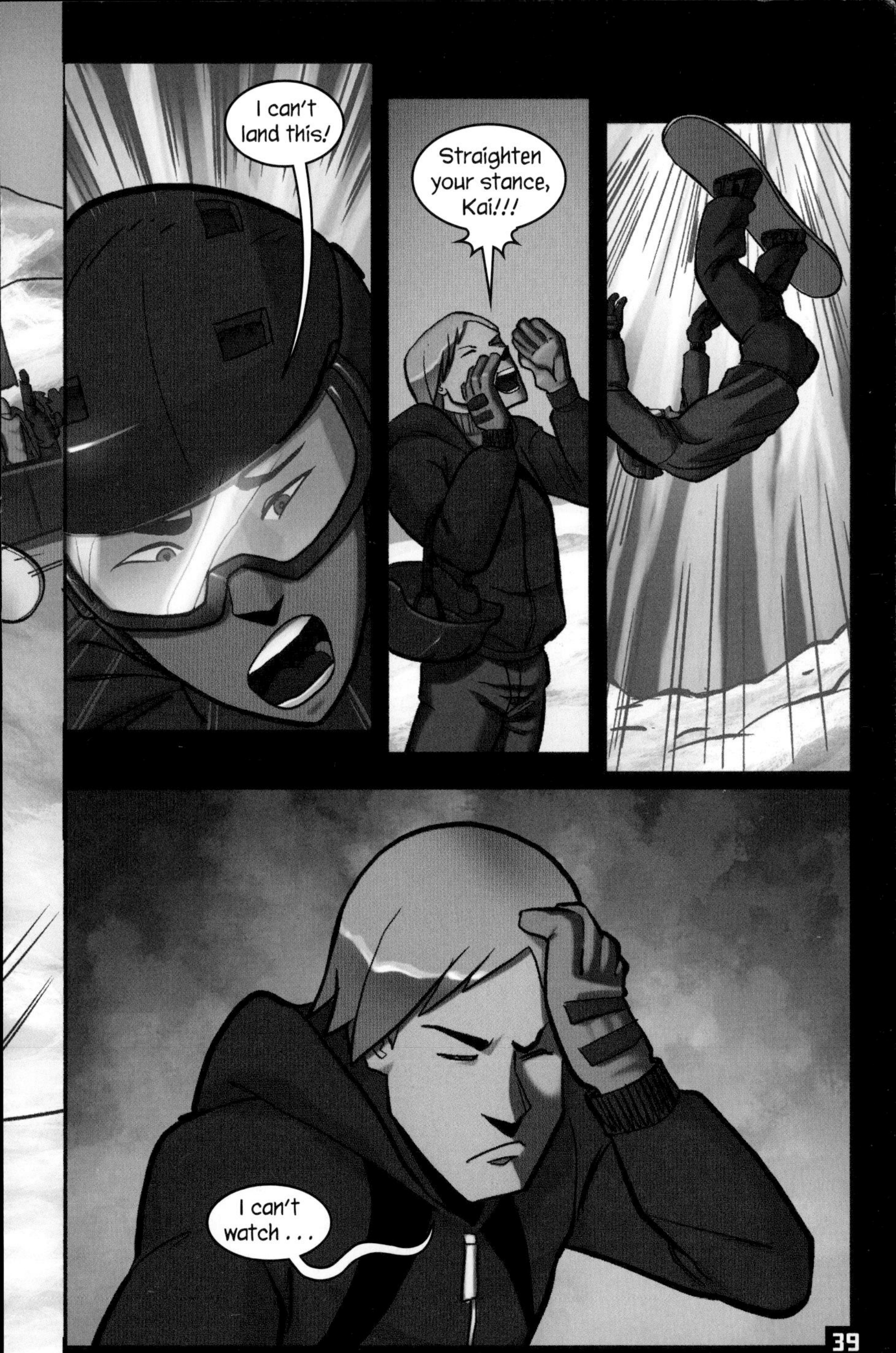
I can't land this!
Straighten your stance, Kai!!!
I can't watch . . .

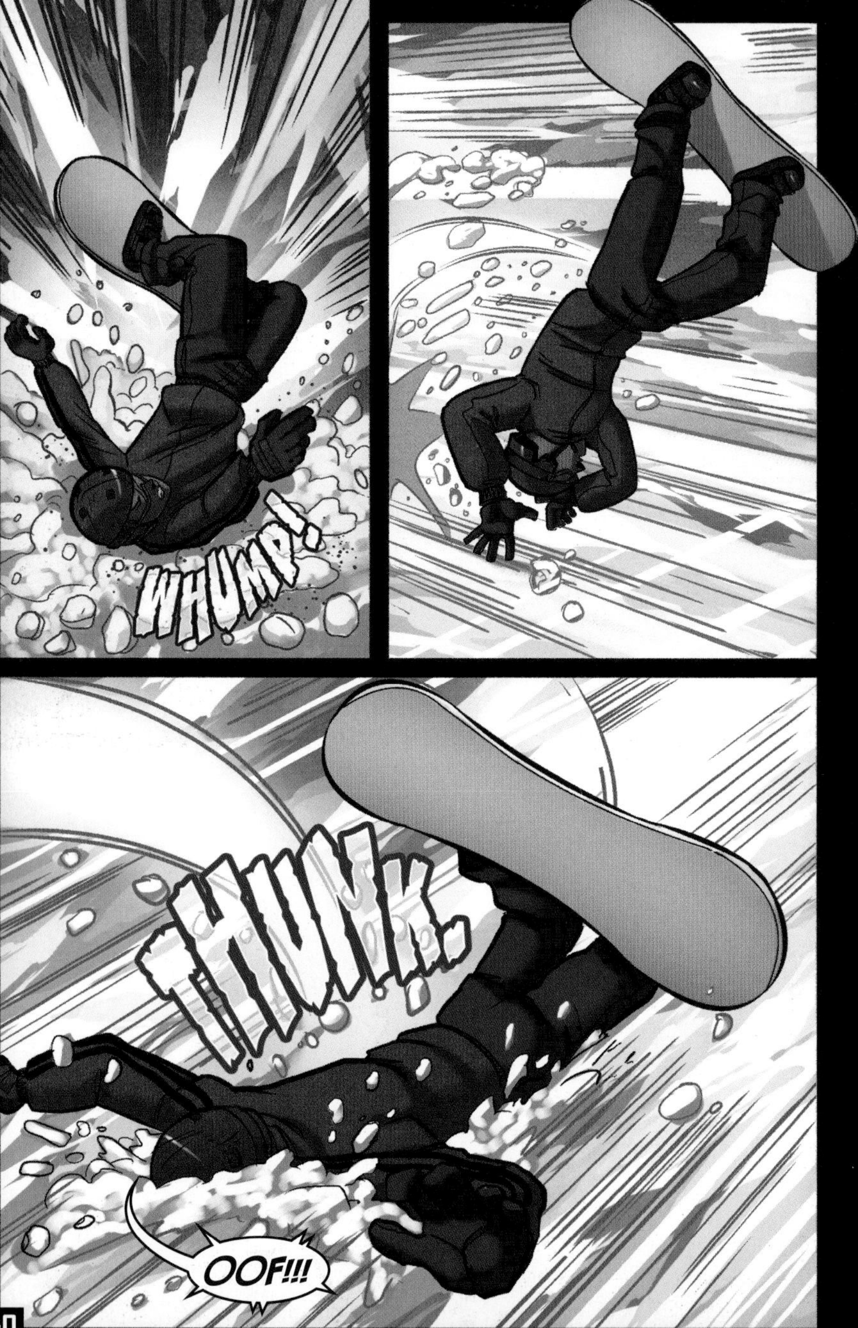
WHUMP!
THUNK.
OOF!!!

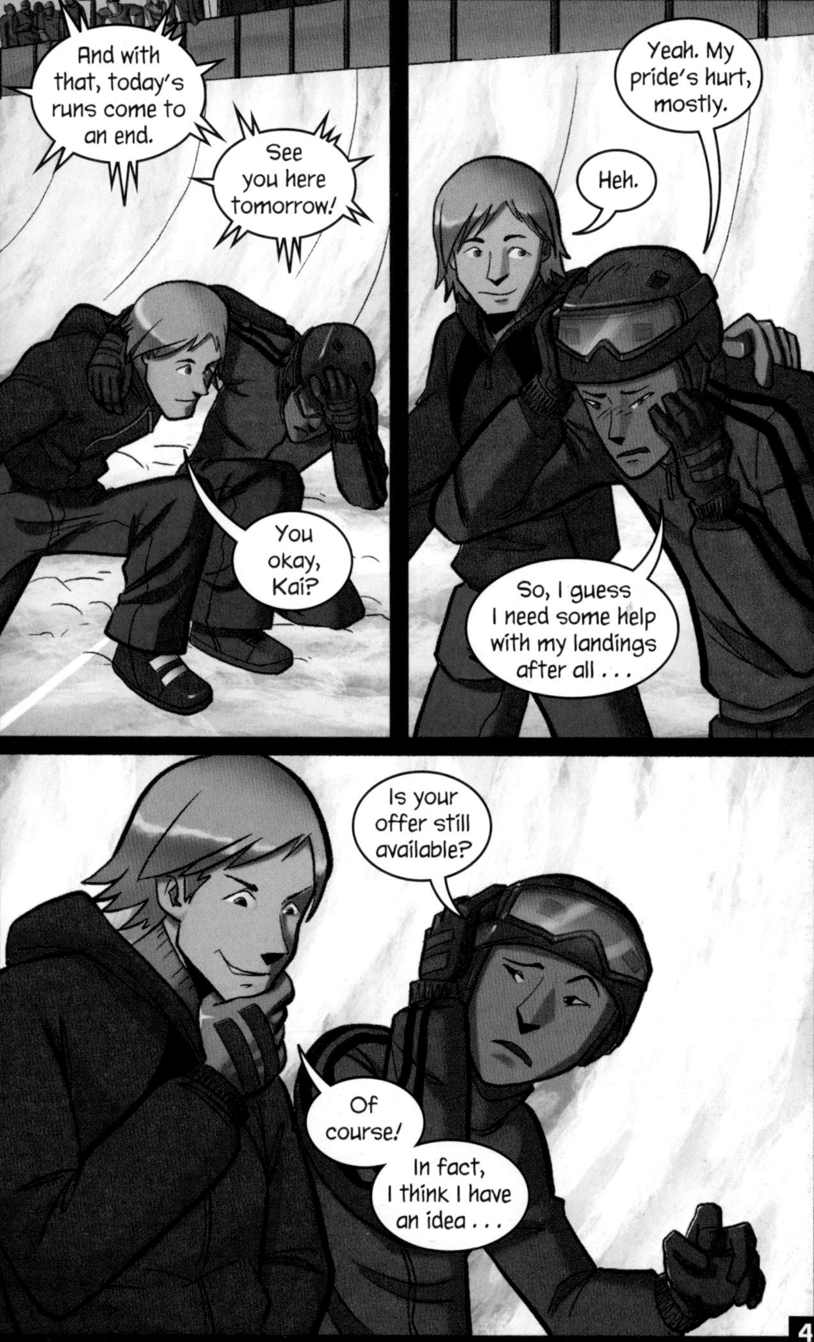
And with that, today's runs come to an end.
See you here tomorrow!
You okay, Kai?
Yeah. My pride's hurt, mostly.
Heh.
So, I guess I need some help with my landings after all . . .
Is your offer still available?
Of course!
In fact, I think I have an idea . . .

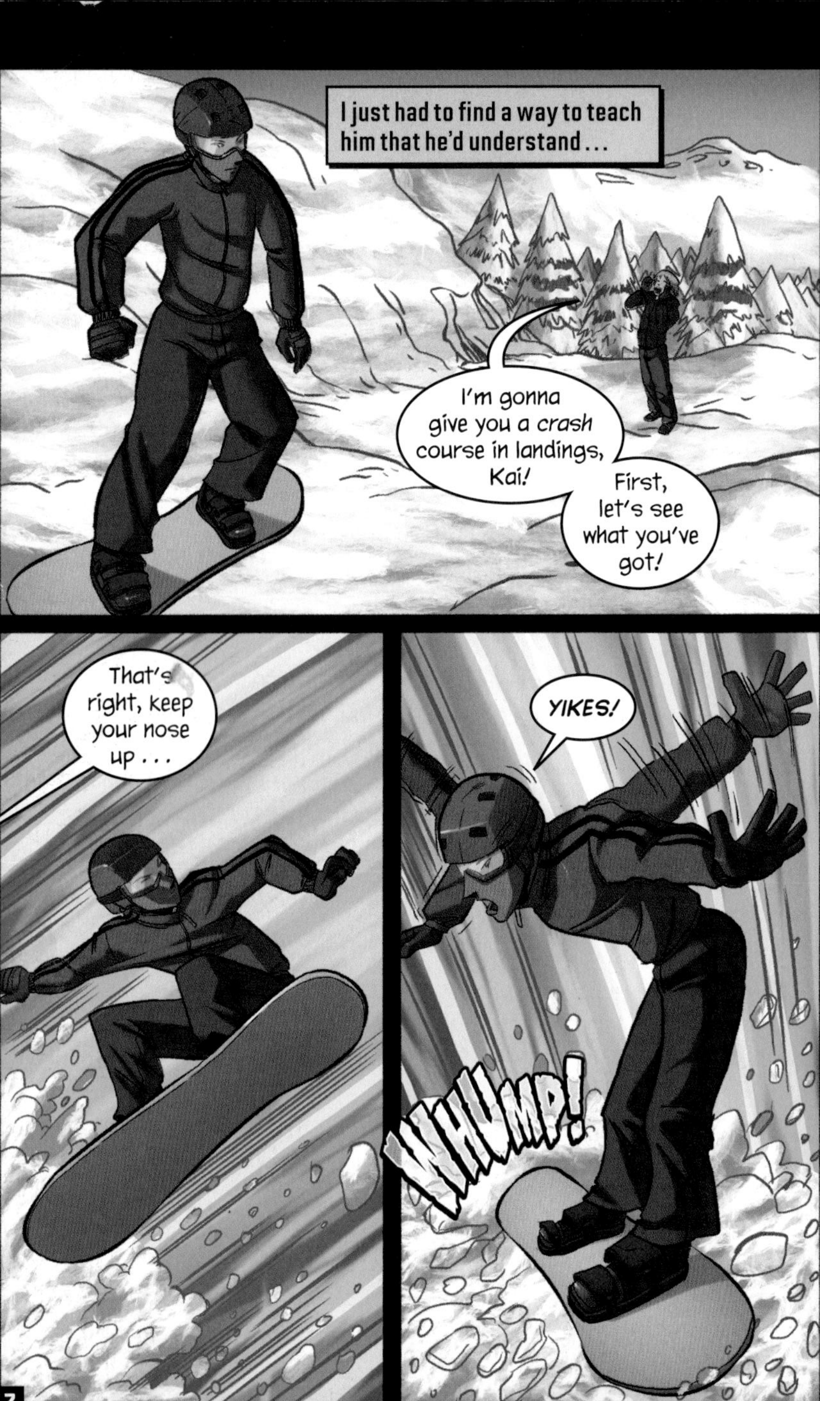

I just had to find a way to teach him that he'd understand . . .
I'm gonna give you a *crash* course in landings, Kai!
First, let's see what you've got!
That's right, keep your nose up . . .
YIKES!
WHUMP!

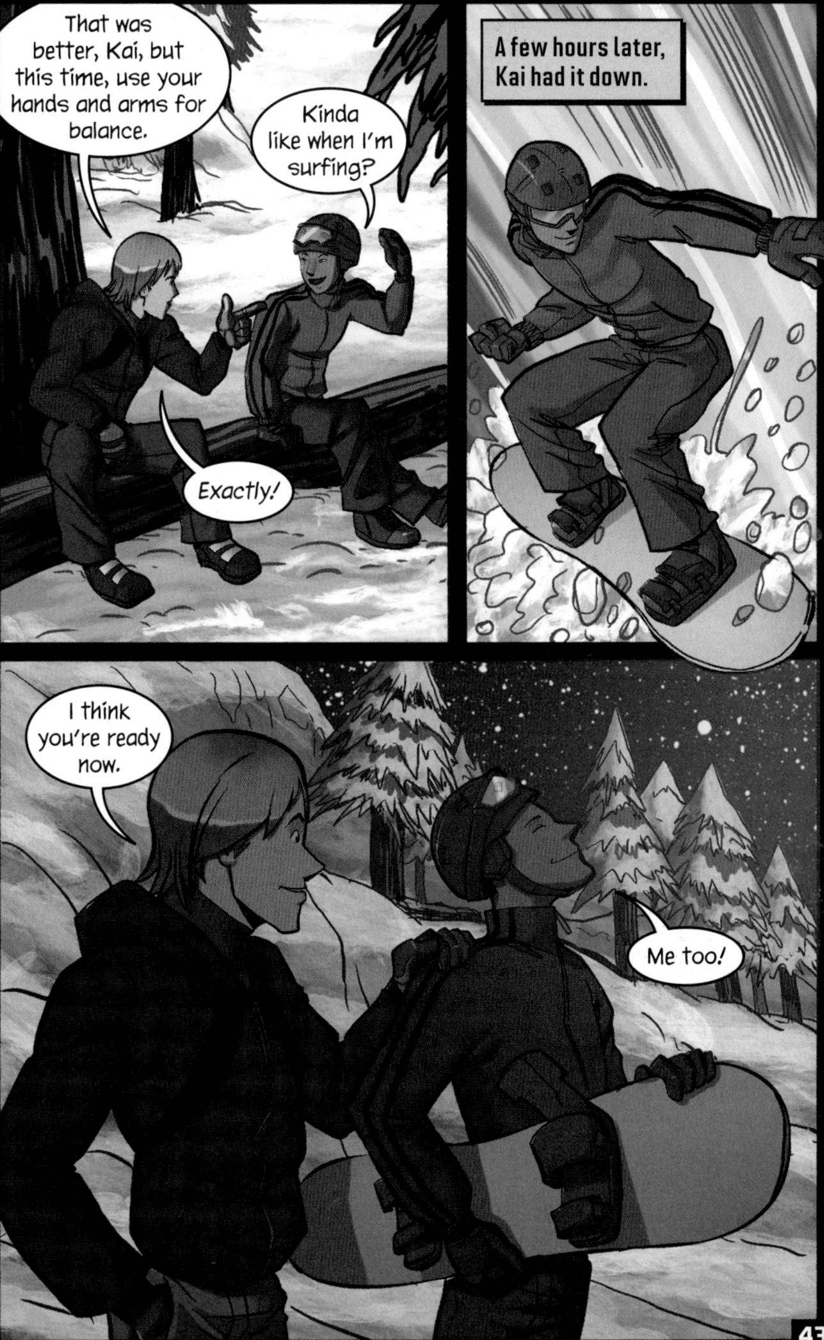
That was better, Kai, but this time, use your hands and arms for balance.
Kinda like when I'm surfing?
Exactly!
A few hours later, Kai had it down.
I think you're ready now.
Me too!

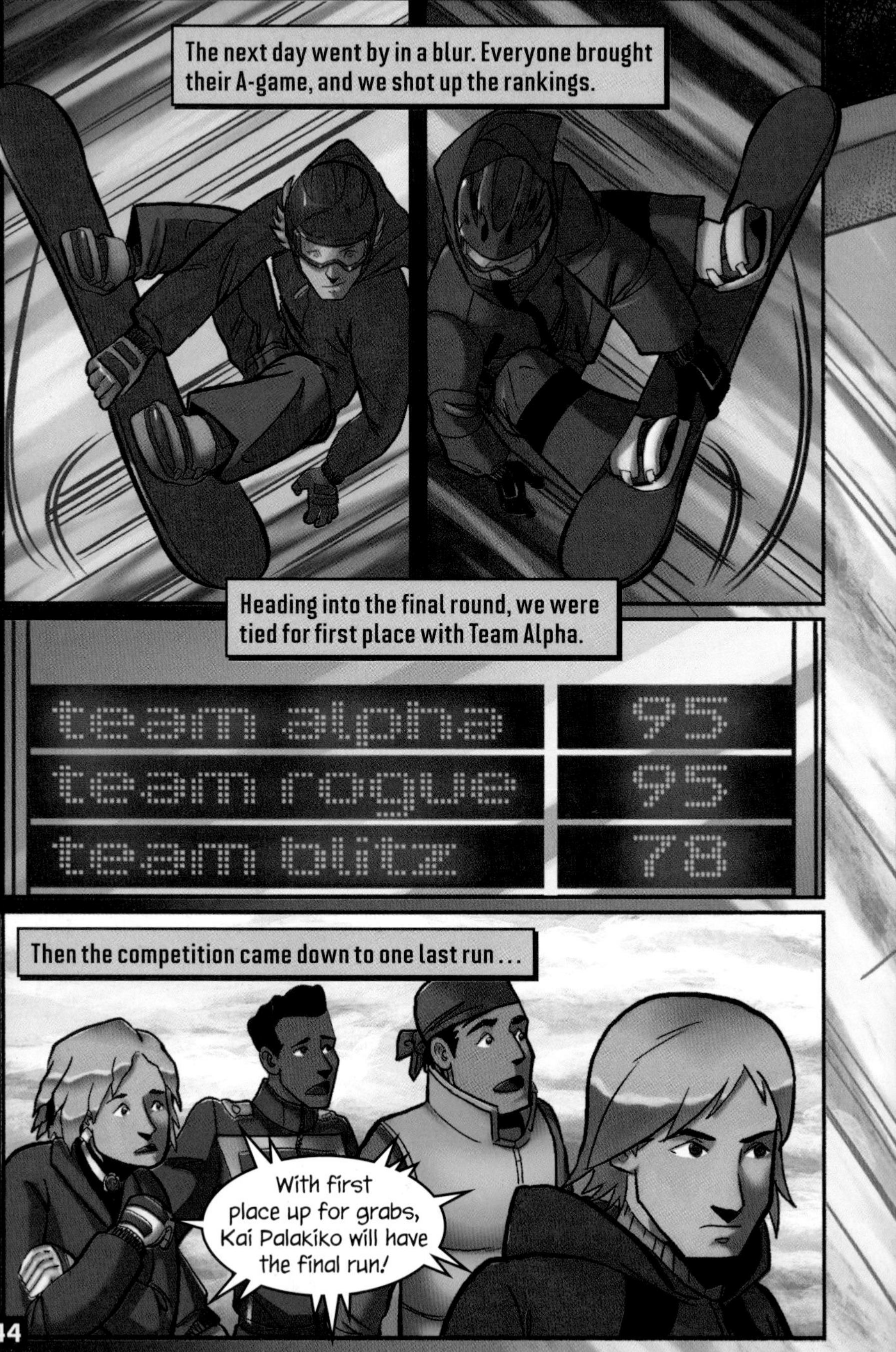
The next day went by in a blur. Everyone brought their A-game, and we shot up the rankings.
Heading into the final round, we were tied for first place with Team Alpha.
team alpha 95
team rogue 95
team blitz 78
Then the competition came down to one last run . . .
With first place up for grabs, Kai Palakiko will have the final run!

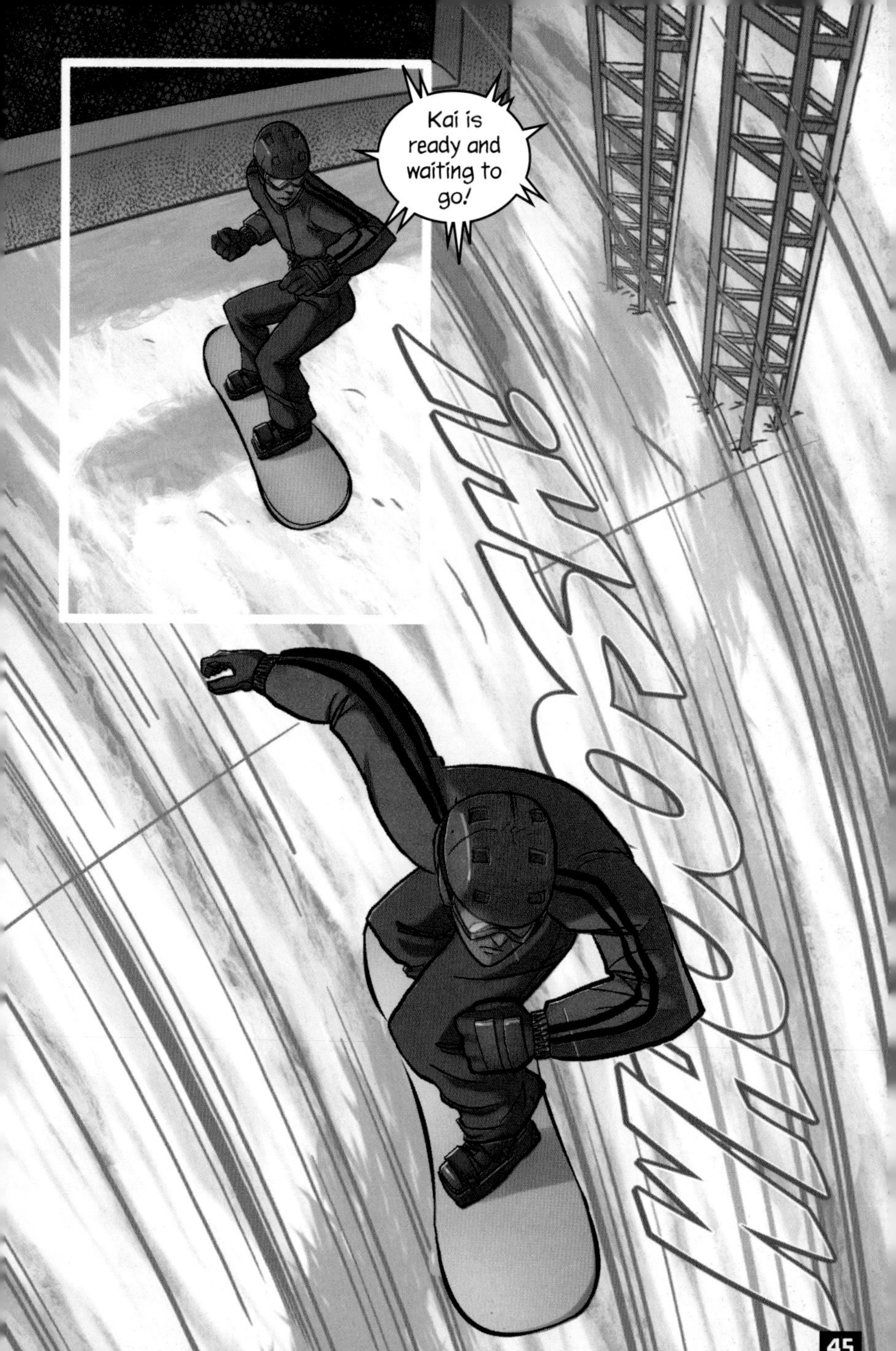
Kai is ready and waiting to go!
WHOOSH!

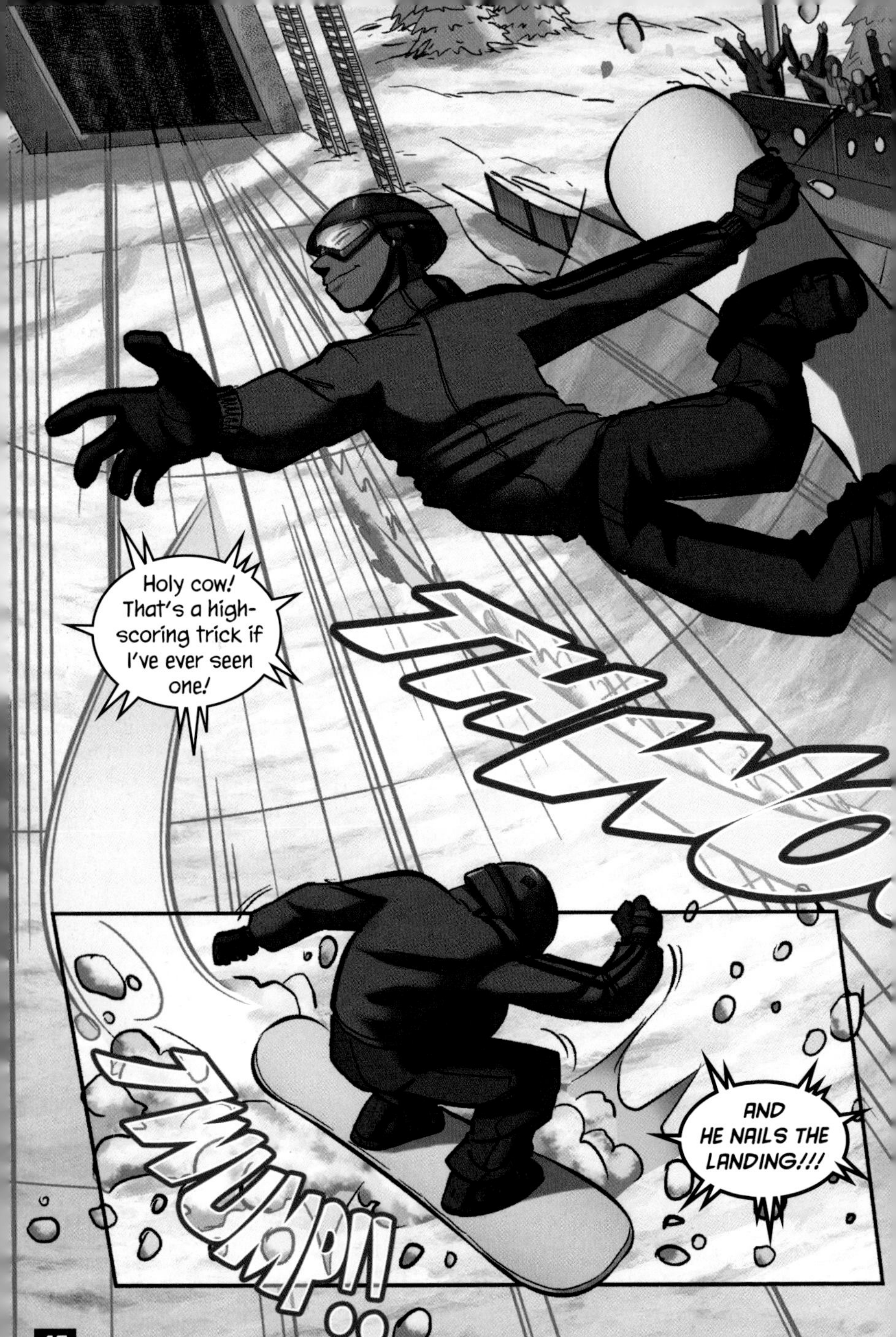
Holy cow! That's a high-scoring trick if I've ever seen one!
AND HE NAILS THE LANDING!!!

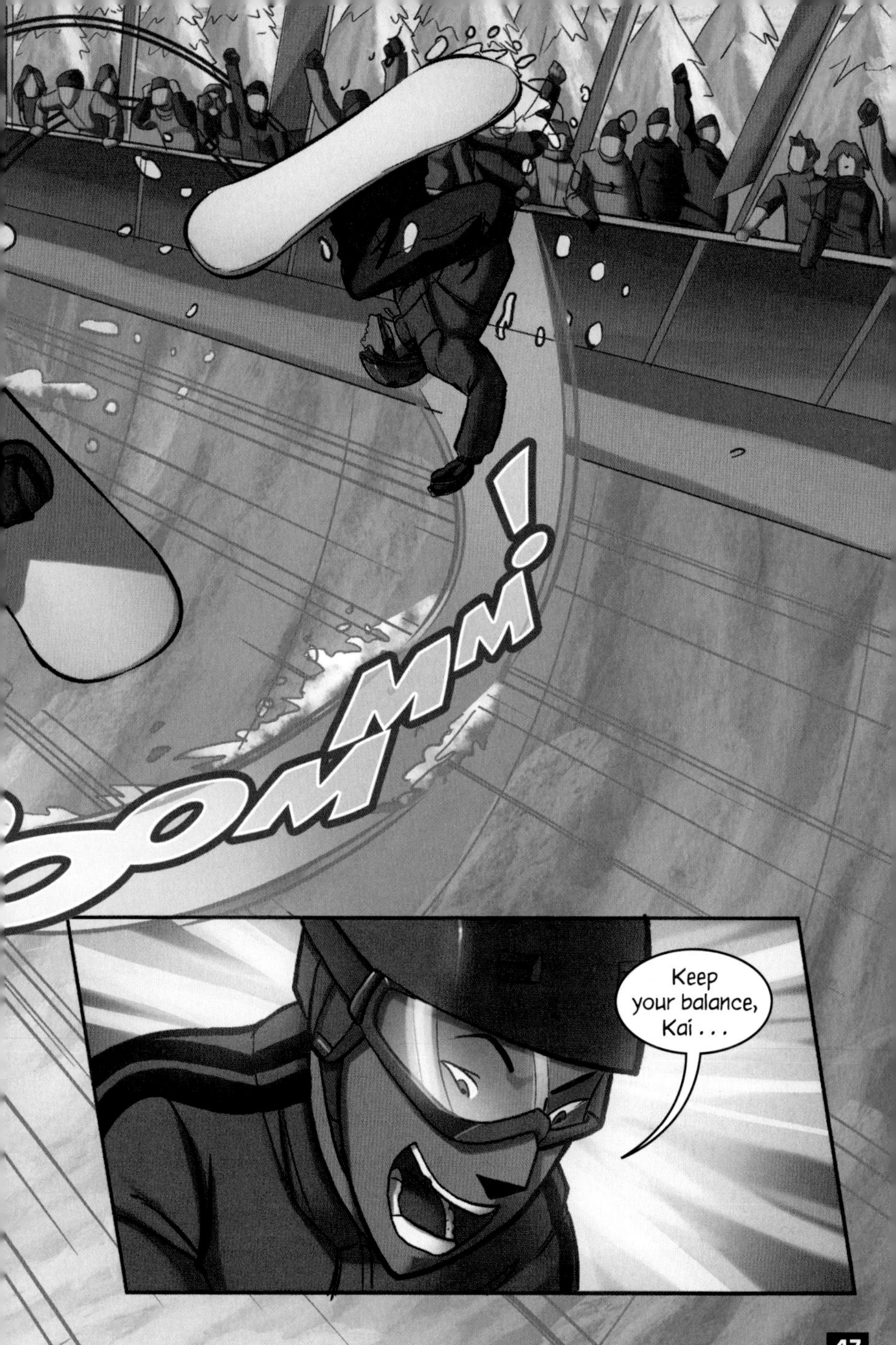
OOMMMM!
Keep your balance, Kai . . .

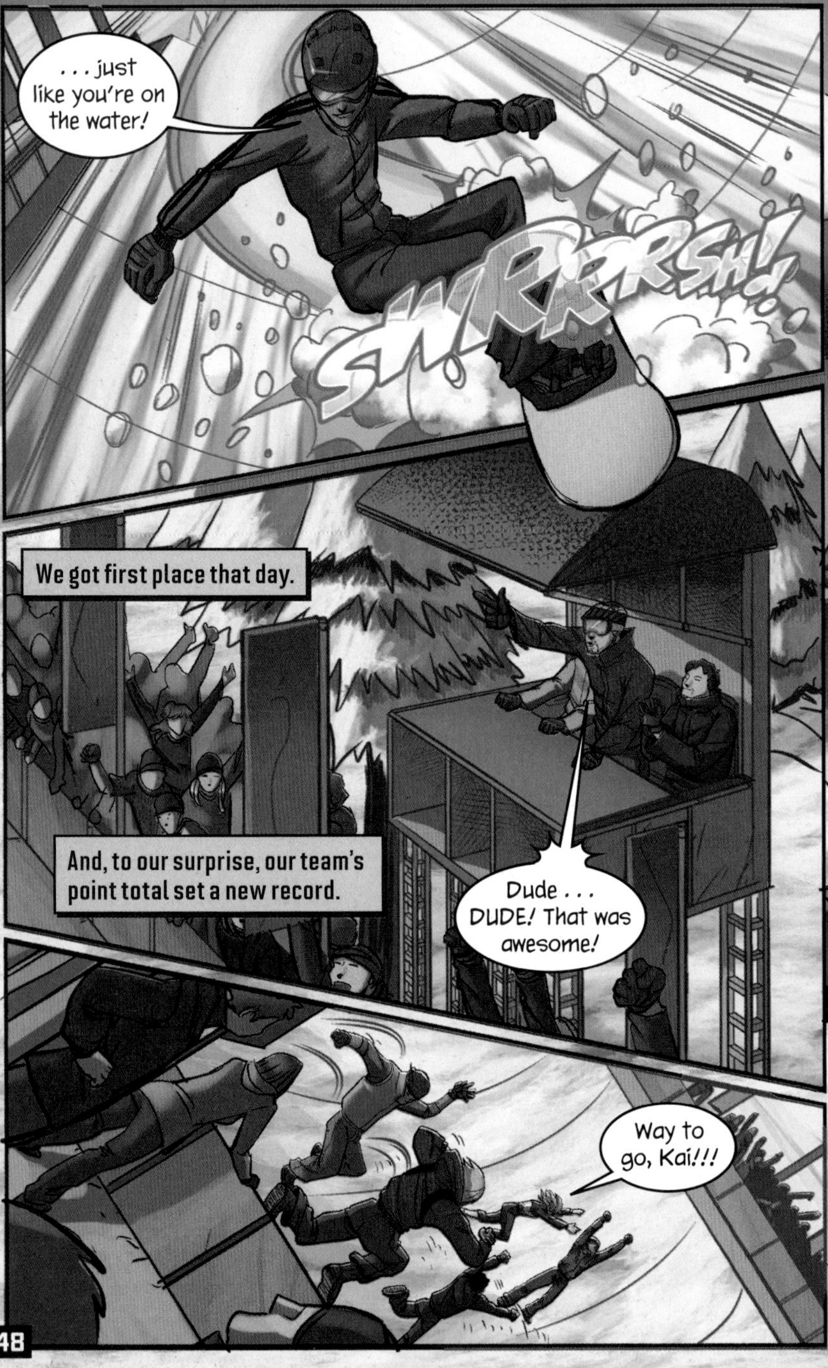
. . . just like you're on the water!
SHHRRRSH!
We got first place that day.
And, to our surprise, our team's point total set a new record.
Dude . . . DUDE! That was awesome!
Way to go, Kai!!!

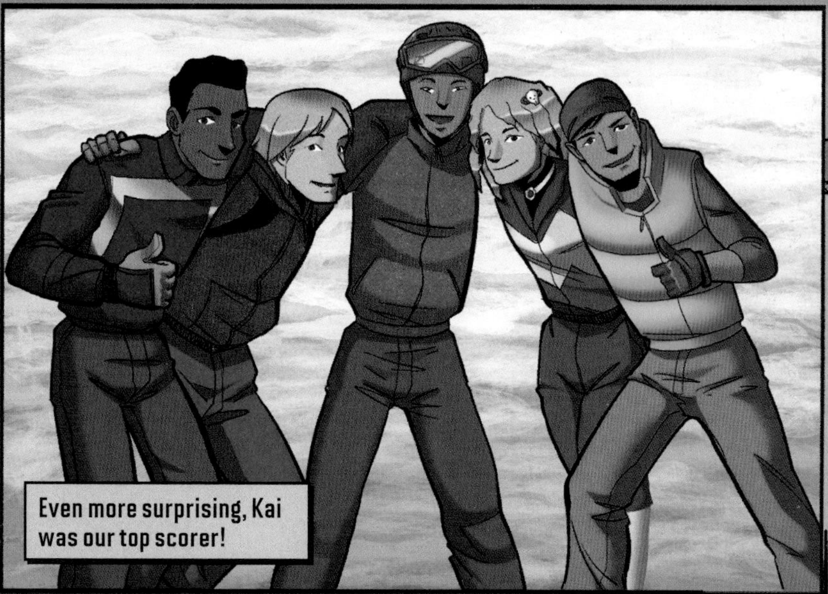
Even more surprising, Kai was our top scorer!

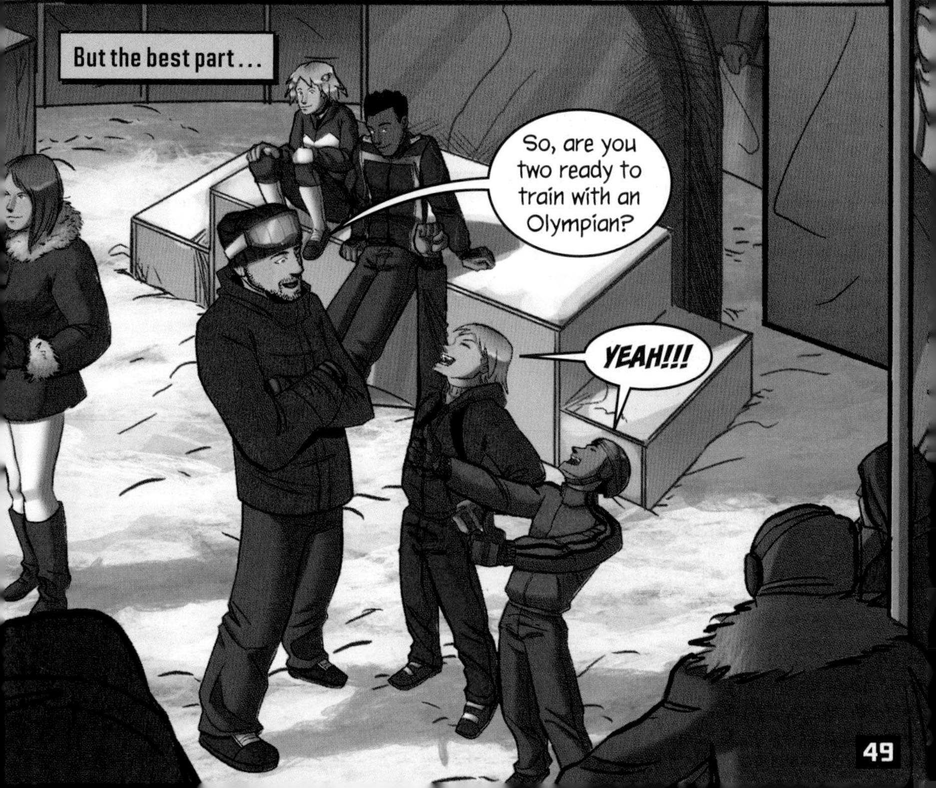
But the best part . . .
So, are you two ready to train with an Olympian?
YEAH!!!

SPORTS ZONE

POSTGAME RECAP

SND
SNOWBOARDING

PNT
PAINTBALL

SKT
SKATEBOARDING

BMX
BMX FREESTYLE

SRF
SURFING

TEAM ROGUE TEAMS UP!

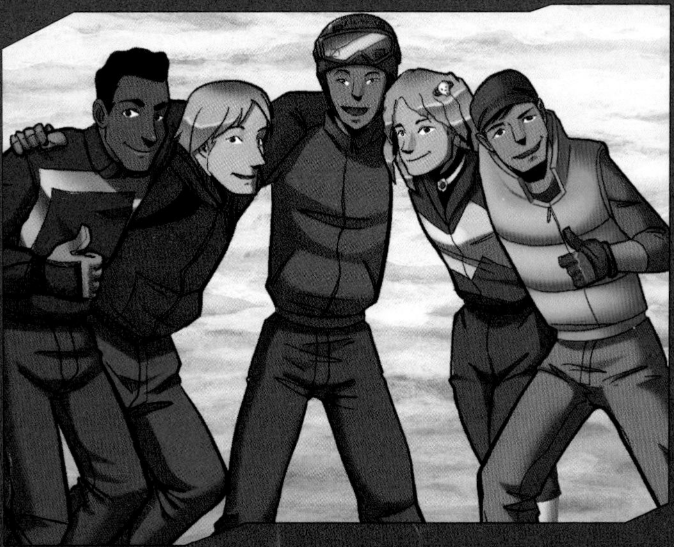

STORY: Isaac Foster and Kai Palakiko ended up making a talented team. With Isaac's instruction, Kai was able to tap into his surfing roots to improve his snowboarding skills. At the same time, Isaac admitted that sometimes you have to compromise. "Everyone's different," he said. "There may be a best way to do things in most cases, but there's always an exception — and Kai is definitely exceptional."

BY THE NUMBERS

TOTAL POINTS:
TEAM ALPHA: 104
TEAM BLITZ: 86
TEAM ROGUE: 105

Sports Illustrated KIDS

UP NEXT: SI KIDS INFO CENTER

POSTGAME EXTRA

WHERE *YOU* ANALYZE THE GAME!

BLZ vs BNS
3-4

TGR vs ROR

EAG vs BAN
14-7

SPA vs WLD
4-3

BAN vs ROR
24-5

ROR vs UG

BLZ vs BNS

Snowboarding fans got a real treat today when Team Rogue took down Team Alpha in a memorable snowboarding battle. Let's go into the stands and ask some fans for their opinions on the day's big game ...

DISCUSSION QUESTION 1

Do you think Isaac handled Kai's problems well? Are there ways he could've been a better teacher? Discuss your answers.

DISCUSSION QUESTION 2

Which sport do you think is harder to learn — surfing or snowboarding? Why?

WRITING PROMPT 1

If you could learn any sport from any professional athlete, which sport and athlete would you choose? Write about it.

WRITING PROMPT 2

Imagine that you're going to start your own sports team. Which four friends will you include? What will your team name be? What will your uniforms look like? Write about your team.

Sports Illustrated KIDS

INFO CENTER

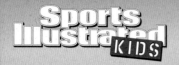

GLOSSARY

COMPETITION (kom-puh-TISH-uhn)—a contest of some kind

CONVINCED (kuhn-VINSSD)—made someone believe you

DOOMED (DOOMD)—destined to suffer a terrible fate

FORFEIT (FOR-fit)—give up

IMAGINED (i-MAJ-uhnd)—pictured something in your mind

IMPRESSED (im-PRESSD)—made people think highly of you

TRANSLATED (TRANSS-late-id)—expressed something in a different way

VISUALIZED (VIZH-oo-uhl-ized)—pictured something in your mind

CREATORS

Scott Ciencin › Author

Scott Ciencin is a *New York Times* bestselling author of children's and adult fiction. He has written comic books, trading cards, video games, and television shows, as well as many non-fiction projects. He lives in Sarasota, Florida with his beloved wife, Denise, and his best buddy, Bear, a golden retriever.

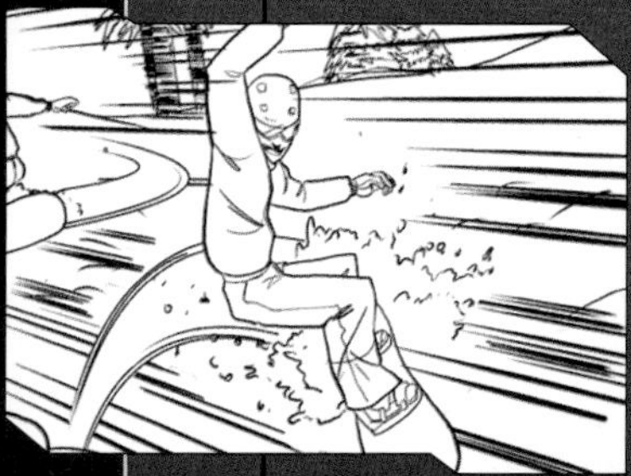

Fabián Cobos › Penciler

Fabián Cobos is a graphic designer and illustrator. He worked in Chiapas for a couple of years on independent comic book publications. Nowadays, he lives in Monterrey, Mexico, where he works with his Graphikslava colleagues as a penciler. He loves alternative rock, sketching people in train stations, and reading historical novels. He doesn't like to eat fish.

Sergio Martínez › Inker

Sergio Martínez was born in Monterrey, Mexico. He studied graphic design at the UANL School of Visual Arts. Sergio has worked as an illustrator, a comic and concept artist for animation, and even as a sculptor. Recently, he joined the Graphikslava team, where he enjoys developing comics for publishers like Stone Arch Books, Marvel Comics, DC Comics, IDW, and many others. He likes to draw. A lot.

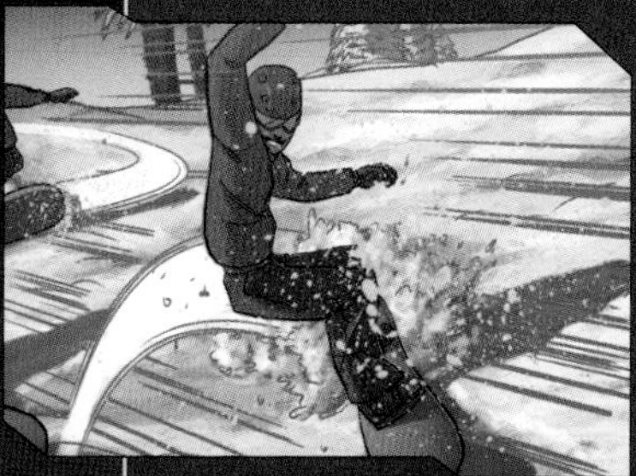

Fernando Cano › Colorist

Fernando Cano is an emerging illustrator born in Mexico City, Mexico. He currently resides in Monterrey, Mexico, where he works as a full-time illustrator and colorist at Graphikslava studio. He has done illustration work for Marvel, DC Comics, and role-playing games like Pathfinder from Paizo Publishing. In his spare time, he enjoys hanging out with friends, singing, rowing, and drawing!

Sports Illustrated KIDS GRAPHIC NOVELS
QUICK COMIC

TONY JAY IN:
AVALANCHE FREESTYLE

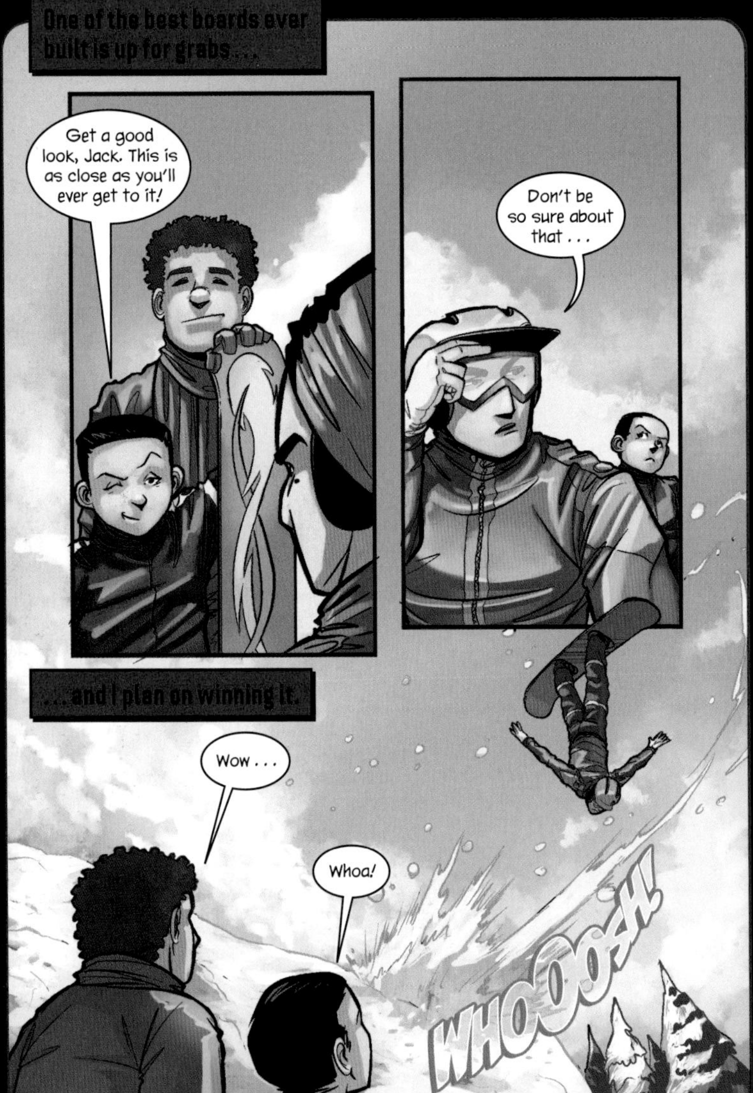
One of the best boards ever built is up for grabs . . .
Get a good look, Jack. This is as close as you'll ever get to it!
Don't be so sure about that . . .
. . . and I plan on winning it.
Wow . . .
Whoa!
WHOOOOSH!

LOVE THIS QUICK COMIC? READ THE WHOLE STORY IN AVALANCHE FREESTYLE – ONLY FROM STONE ARCH BOOKS!

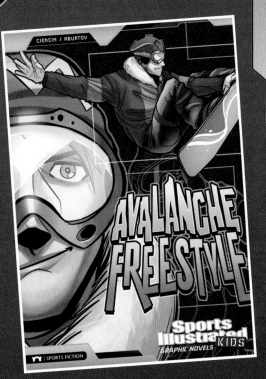

THE FUN DOESN'T STOP HERE!

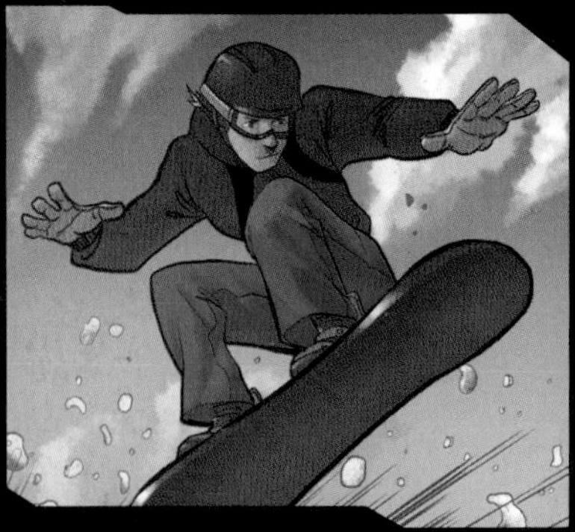

FIND MORE:

GAMES
PUZZLES
CHARACTERS

www.capstonekids.com

Still want MORE? Find cool websites and more books like this one at www.Facthound.com. Just type in the Book ID: 9781434222428 and you're ready to go!

AND FOR SPORTS HEADLINES, SCORES, STATS, PHOTOS, COOL GAMES . . . SIKIDS.com

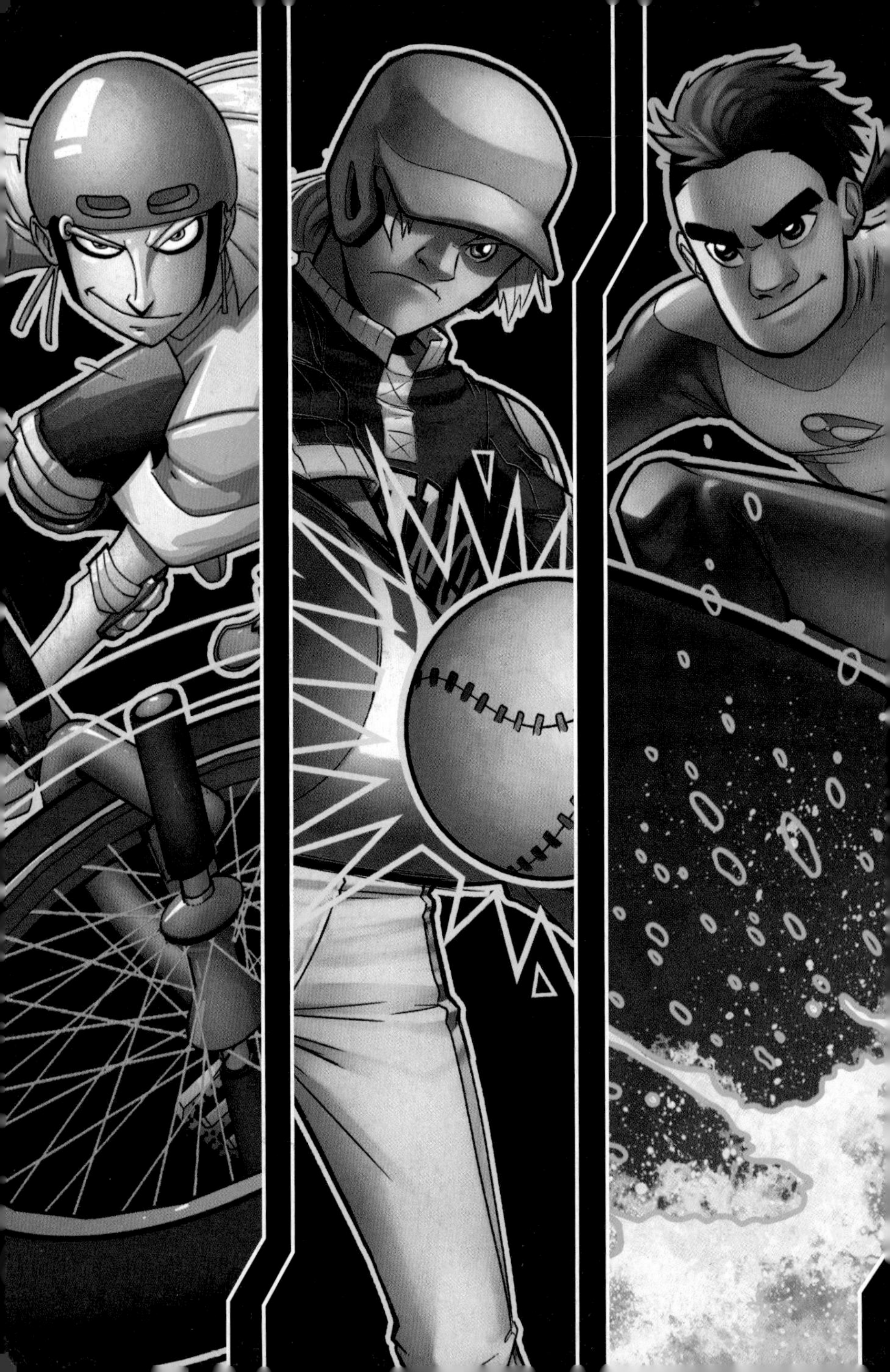

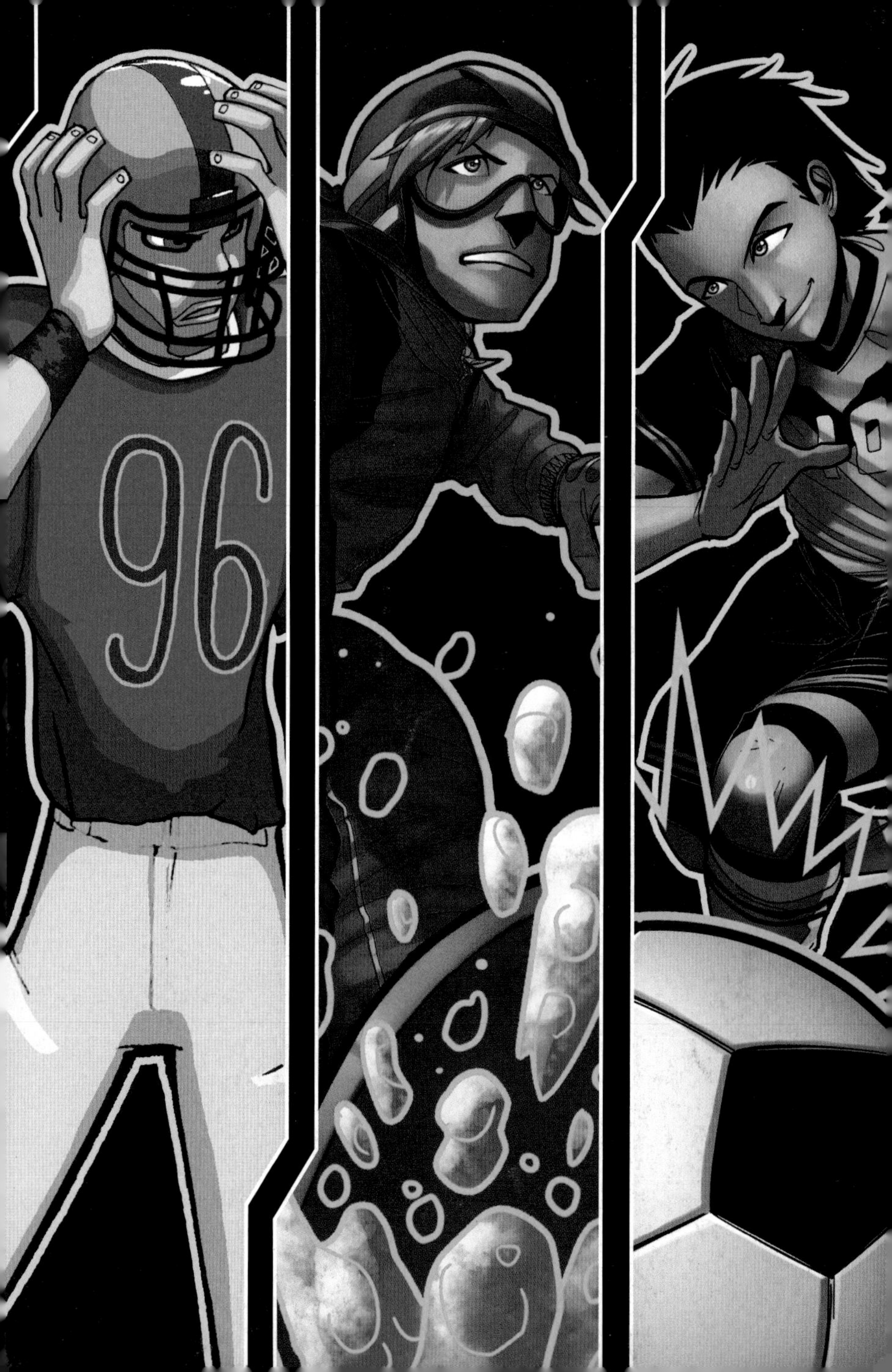

Sports Illustrated KIDS
GRAPHIC NOVELS

STONE ARCH BOOKS
a capstone imprint